Memoirs of a Dead White Chick

Lennox Randon

Library of Congress Control Number: 2015904801
CreateSpace Independent Publishing Platform
North Charleston, SC

ISBN: 1511407042
ISBN 13: 978-1511407045

Cover art design, layout, & artwork by Lennox Randon
Stylized pen concept licensed from JelenaA/Shutterstock.com
www.LennoxRandon.com

To

Lileah & Lether

who always believed in me,

and

to

Lark, Chris, & Page

in whom I will always believe.

Contents

The Letter 1

1   The Accident... 3

2   Maybe Shirley MacLaine was onto Something......... 10

3   Half the Woman I Was (But Twice the Man)........... 15

4   A New Family 23

5   Life as a Stevedore or Lying on the Dock of the Bay 33

6   Veni, Vidi, Vici 44

7   The Elephant in the Room (or Veni, pt. II).............. 63

8   I Meet Harriet Tubman...................................... 69

9   Bodhisattva (or Golden Slumbers) 79

10 Of Human Bondage 91

11 Territorial Marking... 105

12 Bad Things Sometimes Happen to Good People 120

13 Between Scylla and Charybdis............................. 130

14 Out of the Frying Pan 145

15 Osawatomie Brown... 158

16 Life on the Farm 166

17 Pretzel Logic 178

18 The Prince of Beall-Air 186

19 Prisoners, Hostages, and Casualties 191

20 Room Service 198

21 Monday, Bloody Monday 204

22 Playing Doctor 211

23 Shadows 224

24 From the Muddy Banks of the Potomac 235

25 Sweet Caroline 245

26 Family Reunion..254

27 A Drag Race 264

28 When the Snafu Hits the Fan..................................272

29 On the Road Again...285

30 There's No Place Like Home..................................296

31 Epilogue 301

    Afterword 304

Never open the door to a lesser evil, for other and greater ones invariably slink in after it.

Baltasar Gracián, The Art of Worldly Wisdom

The Letter

I hope the paraffin preserved my tablets. No word processor was handy, so you'll have to cope with my longhand.

I am sending this to explain to whomever might care what has happened to me. I would try to publish it now, but my story is too far-fetched to even be considered fanciful science fiction.

In a perfect world, I'll get this document and avoid my untimely death altogether. If not, at the very least, someone will find out the truth regarding the events I unintentionally set in motion.

I am coming to accept that some things are immutable, so I know that this is unlikely to reach me before I die. I don't know if this is a diary or an autobiography or what, but it is my story.

Eleanor

March 30, 1870

1

The Accident

December 1999

It began as one of those days when I asked myself, what else could go wrong?

And then I died.

$\delta\ \delta\ \delta$

The following is my attempt to chronicle what has occurred in the time since my death. If I had known what would follow, I certainly would have chosen to remain dead.

For now, I only know that I need to write about how I ruined everything.

Thousands upon thousands of lives.

I feel responsible. I am responsible.

Whether my story will be accepted as true, I can't say, but please believe me when I say I am profoundly sorry.

Consider this my confessional.

♪ ♪ ♪

The first time I regained consciousness, I looked up into the face of a female paramedic. She had worried green eyes, short brown hair, and a bloody shirt. Big-boned like me, but not soft like I'd allowed myself to become.

After a few seconds, I mustered enough awareness to realize that the blood on her white shirt was mine. A Black male paramedic with a shaved head and goatee was adjusting an IV. Bumpy, zigzaggy ride. Siren blasting. I figured it was pretty bad.

They had immobilized me by strapping me to a wooden backboard. A cervical collar further limited my movement, or at least I hoped that was the cause. An oxygen mask covered my nose and mouth. At least they weren't charging paddles and yelling, "Clear!"

♪ ♪ ♪

I don't remember the exact date, but I know it was a Friday because I recall planning to give a spelling test to my fifth-graders. And it was December. Winter break was coming up and, frankly, I was really looking forward to it.

The tone for my last day of life was set the prior evening when I'd spent over an hour on the telephone

4

with parents, nearly two hours planning the next day's lessons, and another two hours grading papers. I worked as an elementary schoolteacher in Houston, Texas in my "pre-mortem" existence. Teaching was a job with many ups and downs, and I was deeply submerged in a down period.

I entered this most noble profession for a variety of altruistic reasons, but at certain times, it seemed the only reasons for remaining in the business were June, July, and August.

Needing to decompress, I'd poured a small glass of red wine, popped *Pretty Woman* into my Betamax, and stayed up way too late. I fell asleep during the movie, at some point waking up just long enough to turn off the TV.

₧ ₧ ₧

The second time I regained consciousness, the paramedics were unloading my stretcher from the rear of the ambulance. The jolt when the wheels struck the pavement awakened me momentarily from a dream in which I had made it to work just in the nick of time.

I blinked at the paramedics a couple of times, and then drifted back off to take attendance and begin the day's reading lesson.

₧ ₧ ₧

The alarm had gone off right on time that morning, but I'd decided that I deserved five more minutes.

Thirty minutes later, I realized that I'd gotten more than I deserved and I was going to be late for work.

Fortunately, I had a low-maintenance morning ritual. By 7:45, I'd slipped my dainty size tens into my boring but sensible Rockport loafers, gathered all three overstuffed book bags, and plopped into the cab of my trusty pickup truck.

Unfortunately, I had no time for my usual decaf coffee — cream, no sugar — but foregoing the morning java would get me to the school very close to on time. I really hated skipping the coffee, but every minute counts with Houston traffic.

I popped in my current favorite Beatles CD and hit the road. Freeway traffic moved smoothly, and, by the time I reached my exit, I felt optimistic about making it to campus before the morning bell. The light turned green and I began across the intersection, relieved that I wouldn't be too terribly late. George Harrison and Jimi Hendrix were wailing away on their guitars.

When the speeding wrecker ran the red light and slammed into the driver's side door of my truck, all I could think was that I'd probably be late after all.

♪ ♪ ♪

At the time of my death, my name was Eleanor Louise Ross. I was a 41-year-old White female, 5'9" tall, big boned, as I mentioned earlier (family trait), with shoulder-length brown hair and hazel eyes, born and raised in Houston. No distinguishing marks or tattoos.

Although I sometimes had trouble convincing my students (and myself), I spent almost seven years as a police officer before deciding that I'd prefer to discourage people from becoming criminals instead of catching them after they'd already made that career choice. After ten years of teaching, police work sometimes seemed like a lifetime ago.

My twin brother Eliot and I applied to the department when we were twenty, almost on a whim. He stayed on after I resigned, more comfortable in the occupation than I had ever been.

I'd left my life in uniform behind, yet a part of me will always be a street cop. Always keeping my gun hand free, always sitting with my back to a wall, always scanning for the unexpected attack. Ever ready, ever paranoid, rarely completely relaxed.

But I digress. Anyhow, the stupid tow truck obviously made me miss work completely. I imagine the driver was racing to make the scene of another accident, but after our mishap, the jerk probably tried to get the job to haul away what was left of my truck. With any luck, the officer on the scene had known my brother or me, and kicked the driver's ass. I'll never know, but hey, a girl can dream, can't she?

The initial impact rocketed my body straight up to the ceiling of my pickup, despite my seatbelt. My head struck the truck cab's roof, knocking me out and causing the only pain I can remember from the collision.

გ გ გ

The third and final time I regained consciousness before dying, I must have been in either the ER or an operating room. Bright lights were focused on me. Something was jammed down my throat that made me gag and a sharp pain in my chest made me wince. I caught a glimpse of a small crowd of harried medical types hovering above me.

I felt like I should say something to them, but I was foggy and couldn't construct a coherent thought, let alone speak. Besides, with that thing in my throat, the best I could have done was grunt. So I closed my eyes and surrendered, drifting back to the land of Nod where things didn't hurt so much.

გ გ გ

My mother, father, and brother, Eliot, are all dead too.

I'd always fantasized that at some time in the distant future I'd see them at the end of a brightly lit tunnel, or atop Guadalupe Peak, watching me hike through the clouds towards them at the summit.

When Eliot and I were eleven or twelve, we took a family trip to El Paso. We crossed into New Mexico to visit Carlsbad Caverns the first day. The next day, we climbed to the top of Guadalupe Peak, the highest point in Texas. It wound up being more of an uphill hike than a climb. Eliot and I kept saying we thought the peak was just around the next bend. After about fifteen or twenty false peaks, we gave up guessing. I kept a picture on the mantel over my fake fireplace of the four of us posing by the six-foot-tall pyramidal Pony Express monument at the summit.

What impressed me most about the whole trip was how Mom never complained. We were all rubber-legged by the time we collapsed into the car. Eliot and I were already almost as tall as Mom, and much more active, but the hike had us both totally whipped. Dad said he'd have to wait a few minutes for his legs to recover before he could drive. Mom just leaned back and quietly asked what we'd like to do about dinner.

They say bad luck comes in three's.

Though I don't believe in luck, either good or bad, I'd always assumed that Mom and Dad's deaths were one and two, and Eliot's death was number three. Now I figure that Mom and Dad counted as one bad thing, Eliot was the second, and my own death was the third.

ℰ ℰ ℰ

I have no idea what my exact cause of death was.

But I probably should have had my morning decaf after all.

2

Maybe Shirley MacLaine was onto Something

I woke up dead. All pain was gone.

In a burst (for lack of a better word), everything that I had ever experienced flooded my consciousness. Words said in anger, and in love. Old recipes and credit card numbers. Lyrics to Frank Zappa songs and the weather forecast for Sunday, October 13, 1968.

I felt the need to cry and laugh at the same time as memories of sad events and bad jokes simultaneously assaulted me. Truly an indescribable sensation, yet here I am trying to put it into words.

I was in a place of infinite vastness, lacking beginning or end, height, depth, or width.

I flowed forward but had no body or obvious means of self-propulsion.

Despite my incorporeality, I could see swiftly moving bodies of light all around me, and felt certain that I existed only as a light also. We raced in one direction like lemmings on speed, joined from the left and right, above and below, by identical entities who merged with the herd by flashing inward from random points.

Our destination was unclear, but we all seemed to sense that the direction in which we were traveling was the correct one. No effort was required to progress forward, to follow this instinctual, somewhat magnetic, pull.

I surmised that we were on the road to a heaven, hell, or purgatory. Or maybe I was en route to a cosmic recycling center where my memory would be wiped and my essence would be reincarnated. I hoped I'd get to be a dolphin or an eagle, though I didn't get the sense that animals were in this place. Wherever we were headed, this trippy experience emphatically negated my longstanding theory that nothing at all happened after death.

The existence of some form of afterlife was a concept that I reckoned I would soon be forced to accept. Even though I'd considered myself an agnostic since my freshman year of college, the possibility of a heaven for good folks and a hell for bad folks had always seemed like a darned good idea, a comfort when some great injustice occurred to which I wanted to respond with violence.

And on at least one occasion I have wanted to respond with a blind, uninhibited, atavistic violence.

♂ ♂ ♂

Coincidentally, about a year before my own death, my twin brother was also killed in an automobile accident. While Eliot was on duty as a police officer, a drunkard named Blythe ran him down. After being informed, I reduced the five stages of grief to two stages for several months — depression and anger. I alternated between periods of crying and semi-seriously plotting to excise from the face of the Earth the sorry bastard who'd killed my only sibling.

I'd been a police officer long enough not to play mind games with myself and go through the denial or bargaining stages. Dead was dead.

Only after the trial and Blythe's subsequent imprisonment did I finally reach the acceptance stage.

On the night of the accident, Lieutenant Tuttle, the quintessential desk jockey, uncharacteristically pried himself from his desk and commandeered a marked unit to chauffeur him to my apartment to notify me. In all the years I'd known him, I had never seen Tuttle's lower body. He and his desk seemed to be a part of each other, inseparable as a turtle and its shell.

The knock on the door came at about 3 a.m. At first, the pounding felt like part of my dream, but no matter how many times I answered the door, the knocking continued. I answered the dream door what seemed like countless times, letting in everyone I knew and some people I'd only seen in the movies and on TV. I remember hoping that Mel Gibson and Danny Glover would drop by, and when they were the next people to tap on the door, I knew this was a dream and the knocking emanated from a point outside of my subconscious.

Something had to be wrong or a burglar was being awfully cautious before breaking in. I reached into my nightstand drawer and felt for my Smith & Wesson Model 38 revolver. Very little of my paranoia from my days and nights on the police force had dissipated.

I knew how wrong things were when I saw a hangdog Lt. Tuttle through the peephole. He was taller than I thought he would be, and his legs were actually rather spindly for a man of his heft.

He looked past me over my shoulder instead of making eye contact. Once he tried to look at the ground, but quickly averted his eyes rather than appear to be staring at my exposed legs. Tuttle kept saying, "I'm sorry," though he was in no way responsible for the accident.

⚮ ⚮ ⚮

One of the gazillion points of light came at me from my left, just like the speeding wrecker, but this time I sensed its presence and flinched, swerving to avoid contact. I didn't know I could do that — voluntary movement.

While dodging the point of light to my left, I nearly slammed into a point of light to the right just emerging from wherever they came from. Our beams just brushed as I was suddenly sucked into the hole from which the other light had originated.

If I'd been a microsecond sooner, I'd have probably knocked the point of light back into its point of egress. A microsecond later and I'd have hit a wall and continued on my way.

And again I was unconscious.

3

Half the Woman I Was (But Twice the Man)

I awakened as if from a frightening and all too realistic nightmare, sweaty and panicked. A sharp pain assaulted my chest, and inexplicably, I was gasping for air as if I had been underwater too long.

The room was poorly lit, and what light there was flickered like a candle's. Moreover, a thin, pungent blanket pulled over my face diffused the already minimal illumination. Obviously the whole dying and traveling as a point of light thing was a dream.

Then it hit me. *The nurses covered me up because they think I'm dead. I've got to remove this blanket!*

I tried and failed. Despite being unmistakably alive, I was unable to move any of my limbs. I needed to fling off the blanket in order to prove life before they decided to ship me to the morgue or worse.

This utter helplessness heightened the sense of distress brought on by the crazy death dream and provided a nice segue to my desperate, hysterical scream.

My mouth seemed to be my only working body part, other than my brain, but even it was betraying me. An otherworldly, cracking baritone poured through my lips, spooking me even more and prompting me to wail louder. I imagined that I would appear to others like an oddly dubbed movie character, with a woman's lips moving but a man's voice coming out.

My vocalizing must have inspired someone else, for a series of staccato screams interrupted my wailing. The second screamer sounded female and appeared to be hyperventilating (or having an orgasm) as she startled me into silence.

Another female was repeating, "O Lord Jesus," almost like a chant or spell.

A wide-eyed little Black girl of about six or seven pulled back the blanket from my face and said unsurely, "Matthew?"

I furrowed my brow, blinked, and looked back at the girl quizzically. After a few seconds, though, I realized she was talking to me. But why would she call me Matthew?

I scanned the room for a familiar face, but saw only what appeared to be a tragically poor Black family.

Three Black adults, including the screamer and the chanter, and the little girl watched me watch them.

At first, I figured they were the janitors, but that wouldn't explain why they had a child with them. And if they were janitors, they had a great deal of work to do because the room was a smelly mess. Based on my surroundings, it was obvious that I was neither in Intensive Care nor in heaven (unless heaven has been greatly overhyped). And if this was hell, perdition wasn't all it was made out to be either. As far as eternal damnation goes, this was more like Heck.

Confused doesn't begin to describe my state of mind. I'd survived a major collision but my hospital room lacked monitors, charts, and IV poles. Not even a TV. If this was a dream, it was in full 3-D, Technicolor Smell-O-Vision. If it was not a dream, it was definitely time to change my HMO.

A large, rank Black man hesitantly stepped up behind the girl. His hair was unkempt, his shirt, rough and ragged, and a rope held up his tattered trousers. He looked homeless. He paused about a yard from the bed, as if afraid of me. The feeling was mutual if that was the case.

Fearful or not, he looked me straight in the eyes and asked, "Boy, is you okay? Talk to me, boy."

Obviously he was speaking to me, but I wondered about his sanity for confusing me with a boy. Nevertheless, I answered him, in my newly acquired pseudo-basso, "I can't move, sir. Get a doctor, please. And some water."

He looked at me as if concerned about *my* sanity and replied, "We thought you was dead, boy. And even the nigger doctor want money. You know we cain't be getting no doctor for a dead boy."

The screamer interrupted and told the man, "He ain't dead now, so get the doctor. God done give us back our boy."

Needless to say, I was beginning to wonder if I had been placed in a post-op asylum. Even on my absolute worst bad hair day, no one has confused me with a Black boy.

The smelly Black man eased toward the door, but did not leave. His position at my bedside was taken over by an older Black woman. She was less funky than the man, but just as poorly dressed. The old woman put her arms around the little girl's shoulders and slowly eased her away from me.

My whole body tingled like a limb that has fallen asleep, but instead of just an arm or leg, everything was asleep. I closed my eyes to concentrate on regaining my bodily functions. The first sensation I was aware of as my body began to respond, was a mushy wetness beneath my buttocks.

Unable to roll away, I tried to look along the length of my body to make sure I was fully covered. My eyes crossed slightly and I could see my nose.

It was brown. Not a golden-brown, suntanned kind of brown, but an African-American, Negro kind of brown. Right about then, I blacked out.

∂ ∂ ∂

"Is he dead again?" the malodorous man asked from across the room.

"Not yet," I responded in my still-hoarse, gravelly voice. "Was I dead before, and why do you keep calling me boy?"

The screamer spoke up.

"Honey, you was as dead as anybody I ever seen, but the good Lord musta decided it weren't your time. And your Daddy has always called you boy, baby. We know you pretty much a man now, but you always gonna be our boy."

Okaaay. I felt certain now that I was in an asylum, or a remarkably vivid, scratch-and-sniff dream.

"So you, ma'am, are my mother?" I asked, playing along with the madness.

"Momma," she corrected, nodding.

"And you, sir, are my father?"

"Daddy, boy," he corrected.

"And who am I?"

"You are Matthew Little," my new mother said. "Don't you remember nothing, honey?"

"I remember a wreck, and an ambulance ride, and a hospital, and dreaming about lights."

My audience looked at me as if I were speaking another language. I decided to change the subject until I could figure out more. Clearly, I wasn't in Texas any more, to paraphrase Shirley Temple from *The Wizard of Oz*. I wish I had a Toto to share this with.

"What day is it?"

"Sunday, boy," the man answered.

Based on everything I had observed so far, I decided to ask a question that I wasn't sure I wanted the answer to.

"I know this is going to sound strange, but what year is it?"

"It 1858, dummy," the girl said with a smile. "You 'member you turned sixteen?"

That would have been a good time to faint, but I'd already done that.

"And where am I exactly?"

My new mother looked at me with a mother's concern, but answered, "You at home, on Walnut Street."

"What city?"

"We still in Philadelphia, baby, just like we always been."

I desperately wanted to discount everything I'd just been told, but I couldn't deny the brown nose that I'd seen with my probably no-longer hazel eyes.

First things first. Health and hygiene.

"I'm having trouble moving and could use some help cleaning up. Would one of you maybe get a towel or something?"

Momma leapt at the chance to do something and began my cleanup, after which I truthfully claimed fatigue and fell asleep.

∂ ∂ ∂

When I awakened again, the man was gone and the older woman was seated at a table across the room. The girl was seated on the floor staring at me.

So much for it being a medication-induced dream.

Momma was seated on the end of the bed, also staring. When she saw me open my eyes, she spoke.

"I prayed hard as I ever prayed before, Matthew. And Jesus answered my prayers and brought you back. He knew I just could not lose another child."

Poor woman, I thought. She did lose another child, but it would be insensitive of me to reveal that so soon. Maybe she'll figure it out herself.

"What happened to me?" I asked. "What was wrong with me?"

"Nobody know, boy. One day you was fine, and then you started throwing up and got the backdoor trots. Anything you ate or drank came back out, one way or the other. Now look at you. So small. You think you can eat something or drink something now?"

"Maybe just a little water first, ma'am. Thank you."

Momma and the little girl shared a confused look, but she stood and poured a cup of water from a pitcher.

The water was warm but felt good. I sipped at first, waiting for a reaction. When nothing bad happened, I gulped the rest.

We waited a bit longer, and when I kept down the water, Momma gave me another glass, this time with sugar added.

♪ ♪ ♪

Funny, the things life will throw at you.

One night you're sipping a glass of Merlot, watching Julia Roberts and Christopher Reeve go on a shopping spree on Rodeo Drive.

The next day, you're a middle-aged dead White chick in the body of a teenaged Black guy in 1858.

Huh. Go figure.

4

A New Family

So, there I was, a dead White chick in the body of a 16-year-old Black male in 1858.

While I lay in bed recovering on stained sheets with a double-digit thread count, I had plenty of time for omphaloskepsis (navel gazing — I'm a bit of a logophile) and to contemplate my situation. Somehow, I had traveled through time, like Marty McFly or some H. G. Wells character.

How the heck does something like that happen, and how do I fix it?

First off, I asked myself, what do I know about time travel?

Isaac Newton said time is an arrow that only goes forward. No backsies. So, no help there.

Recently (in my old life), some scientist guy won a big science prize for sending something a few seconds into the future. Since I was in the distant past wanting to go into the future, such a device would be handy. I just needed the requisite equipment and knowledge. And a heckuva lot of tiny little time jumps.

One of my brighter students last year, Christopher Rhodes, wrote a brilliant paper on Albert Einstein which took me to the precipice of understanding the theory of relativity. In the paper, Chris quoted old Albert as saying time is like a river. He also said that Mr. Einstein proved that time is relative, and ultimately felt that the past, present, and future all occur simultaneously.

That actually fit with the huge tunnel thingie I was in with the other points of light after I croaked, and likewise with me popping up in the past. If all time exists concurrently, theoretically Matthew could die in 1858 and I could die in 1999 without there being any lapse in time between the two events.

But what happened to me was not exactly time travel. At least, not like in a time travel movie where I could hop onto a machine and return to my old body in my own time. That body was long since buried or cremated. Or maybe not, if time is concurrent.

My head was spinning.

I had to die to get here, so that meant I'd have to die to return. And then I'd have to navigate to an unmarked spot in a vast area, and time my ingress to my other essence's egress to get back to my old body.

Beyond impossible.

What happened to me was a one-in-an-umpteen-gazillion accident.

I was stuck.

♂ ♂ ♂

Within two days, this young *male* body was strong enough to move about. While Momma, Daddy, and Grandma went to work, I stayed home with my new little sister, Oleta.

She started in on me as soon as the door latch followed Grandma out of the room. (After spending more time in this era, I noticed there were no doorknobs. I never would have guessed they hadn't been invented by 1858.)

"How did you get inside Matthew's body? Can you get in mine? What's your name? Where is Matthew? Did you kill him? How come —?"

"Whoa. Wait a minute," I interrupted. "One question at a time. Truthfully, though, I'm not sure I can answer some of your questions at all."

Oleta studied me, her face clearly communicating her uncertainty about whether to trust anything I might say. With her eyes squinted, her wild, tangled mat of dirty hair, and her rail-thin body, I felt as if I were being scrutinized by a bird's nest atop a sapling wearing a tattered nightgown. Why any self-respecting sapling would wear such shabby garb is beyond me, but that is the image she conjured in my transmigrated, recovering-from-death, 19th century disease-ravaged mind.

I saw no fear. She was lead detective in the interrogation room, or perhaps a skeptical Oprah Winfrey or Martin King conducting an interview on either of their talk shows.

"I don't know where your brother is for certain. I guess he's in heaven. But I did not kill him, and I don't think I can get inside anyone else's body."

Oleta scrunched her face again and asked, "You didn't know Matthew, did you?"

"No. Why?"

"Well, you said he's in heaven," she replied, raising her eyebrows and giving me a somewhat sad smile. Something in that look and her frank divulgence let me know she believed as much as she could for the present.

We looked at each other for a few moments, not sure where to take the conversation. Oleta's exceptionally bad hair day prompted me to break the silence by asking, "Do you have a comb or brush?"

"Yeah, but you gonna break'em if you try to use'em on Matthew's cockleburs," she teased with a less sad smile.

"Actually, I was thinking about using them on the head of a pretty little girl."

"Who?" she asked innocently, missing my attempted compliment.

"You."

That brought out a full smile, and I saw the pretty girl to whom I had alluded. Oleta beamed while she gathered the comb and brush and a pan of water. After giving them to me, she cocked her head and squinted at me again.

"Are you a girl?"

I had assumed that since she knew I was not Matthew, she also knew I was a woman. I'm no Michelle Pfeiffer, but my femaleness has never been questioned (femininity is another matter).

"I was," I answered in Matthew's baritone, wistfully remembering my breasts.

The twins were all original factory equipment. Certainly, they were cumbersome at times, like when traversing the obstacle course or climbing the rope at the police academy. But it felt odd not having them.

There was a time in my early teens when I didn't feel very good about myself, but my breasts buoyed my self-esteem. My more petite, less well-endowed friends were jealous of them, and, horribly, that made me feel better. Guys seemed to find them interesting even if they found nothing else interesting about me. They were my entrée to a short-lived popularity, until the prettier girls caught up.

I guess a guy would get similarly nostalgic about his penis, if he found himself in a similar situation occupying a female body. I couldn't say for sure, though I supposed I would gain a little insight soon.

Oleta paused, tilted her head, and studied me as if to find some physical sign of my former gender. Logically, however, was it really my *former* gender if I am still a female in my mind and heart, despite my chest and genitalia? A question to ponder.

"We better not tell nobody about that," she suggested. "Daddy and Grandma already think you might be a haint, or least a little crazy."

I tried to brush her hair, but the brush bristles made no headway with her prodigious tangles. After several minutes of negligible progress, Oleta recommended that I use the comb and water.

"Were you a White girl?" she asked, impressing me with her perceptiveness.

"Yes. A White woman, actually."

"Well, we for sure better not tell nobody then," she stated quite seriously and without explanation.

I found that if I used the water liberally, I could loosen the matted hair with my fingers and then comb through small portions of Oleta's hair. Each time I got two sections combed through thoroughly, I twisted them together into plaits like I'd seen some of my Black female students wearing.

"Did you have any sisters?" Oleta asked.

"No. Just a brother. Actually, he was my twin brother."

She thought about that for a few seconds and then asked, "Was he White too?"

I smiled at the question and realized that, considering the circumstances, it wasn't as odd of a question as one might first think.

"Yes, he was. And so were our parents."

"I never talked to a White person before. I seen'em, but they kinda scare me."

"Why? Did they ever do something to you or your family?"

"No, but Grandma says to be careful cause they might snatch me up and send me down South to be a slave. Momma says Grandma just spooking me, but I still get a little scared."

"Probably good advice. I don't know much about what happens here, but better safe than sorry."

"Yeah. Did your parents have slaves?"

"No. We didn't have slaves. Actually, one of my best friends was Black."

Oleta looked at me quizzically. "Black?"

"Negro. Where I'm from, Negro and Black mean the same thing."

"Oh."

For the next hour and a half as I worked on her hair, Oleta and I chatted about my former life and her present life. I avoided any mention of the future or time travel for now. She seemed a bright and understanding child, but truthfully, I was still trying to wrap my own mind around it.

When I was done with her hair, Oleta was pleased and wanted to play. My body, however, insisted I rest, so I did.

ꝸ ꝸ ꝸ

Over the next two days, Oleta and I bonded, sister to sister, or sister to brother, or some combination thereof. She told me a few things about Matthew that I might need to know, and I told her about all the things she could do if she went to school.

I decided that I would make it my business to see to it that she got educated, hoping to pass on my love of words and reading to her. Although she was not required to go to school, I felt that she should attend for as long as she could.

Once a teacher, always a teacher, I guess.

I began teaching her the alphabet and basic addition. Oleta agreed to participate, in large part, I suspect, to humor me.

She was neither exceptionally bright nor dim. Oleta was a classically average student with an indifferent but tolerant attitude about learning. She did not seem to truly accept that an education could help her, and would not believe me when I told her that a Black person could do anything that a White person could do.

By the age of six, she was already convinced of the futility of trying to be anything more than her parents were. Her self-image was low and bound to go lower without education. The undivided attention from me, I believe, contributed to her agreeing to go to school if I could get her into one.

I remember as a girl hearing the James Brown song, "Say It Loud (I'm Black and I'm Proud)" and wondering why someone should be proud of his or her skin color. It was not an accomplishment, but merely what was. Only now did I realize that the song was perhaps really saying, "I'm Black and I'm Not Ashamed of That Fact, and I'm Not Inferior to Anyone Solely Because of the Color of My Skin." Of course, that song probably wouldn't have been as big of a hit, and would have been hell to dance to.

When we weren't studying, Oleta filled me in on who Matthew Little was. Young Matthew was, among other things, a dummy with a girlfriend, a job on the docks with Daddy, and a penchant for slugging his little sister on the arm if she tattled.

I confess to being momentarily intrigued by the possibilities of a girlfriend, because, hey, who goes to Disneyland without getting on the rides. In the end, though, I decided that I did not want to alter history by procreating, assuming the relationship was even at that level. Furthermore, I could not be certain how long I might be here and would not wish to be an absentee parent.

The best strategy, it seemed, would be to terminate the relationship as soon as possible. Who knew that would be the easiest thing I had to do as Matthew?

Within days of my resurrection, the girlfriend sent a message through Momma that she was afraid I was a haint and did not wish me to call on her any longer. My response, sent via Momma, was simply, "I understand. Good luck with the rest of your life."

For the first time since I'd been Matthew, Momma looked at me like I truly was a haint, but agreed to relay the message.

A few days later, when I felt strong enough to go outside for a very short walk, Oleta pointed out Matthew's ex. I had wondered if my lack of protestation at being dumped would affect her self-esteem, but all wondering ceased when I saw her. She strolled down the street alongside a man considerably older than herself, beaming and engaged in an unequivocally amorous clench. Clearly she was proceeding apace with her love life.

As Oleta and I climbed the steps to our porch, my new sister took my hand. Then she looked up at me and asked simply, "Why you think you here?"

I had no answer.

5

Life as a Stevedore or Lying on the Dock of the Bay

Daddy had no doubt as to why I was here.

He brought up the matter of my employment at the end of the eighth day of my new life. He basically stated that the household needed my income, so I had better show up for work on Monday.

By this time I was taking short walks and staying awake for eight or nine hour stretches. While I was in no hurry to engage in manual labor, I was curious about seeing more of the outside world, as well as feeling an obligation to contribute to the family's subsistence. Moreover, it would give me a chance to begin investigating schools for Oleta.

The outside world reminded me of an old Western movie with thousands of extras and the pervasive aroma of manure, river water, human and animal perspiration, and more manure. After being mostly homebound, the nominally fresh air was invigorating, albeit a bit foul. The noises of horses clopping, wagon wheels squeaking, people talking and shouting, and workers hammering made it even more real to me that I truly was alive and residing in Philadelphia in 1858.

Daddy and I walked side by side along the streets up to the docks. Daddy only talked to respond to my questions. I believe that he still felt I was a haint, but he couldn't express it because Momma was so glad to have Matthew back.

When pressed for my job description, he said, "If they picks you, you either takes stuff off the boat or puts things on the boat."

"What do you mean, if they pick me?"

"Well, you ain't been around lately, and you kinda skinny still. And you know they picks men before they picks boys."

"Fair enough," I said, silently hoping I wouldn't have to work too hard this first day out. I did wonder, though, if tales of my death and resurrection might affect my positioning in the labor queue. I posed this concern to Daddy.

"White man don't know and don't care, long as you do the work. Nobody else gonna say nothing 'cause you my boy." He paused for a moment and then added, "That ole girl of yours was just ready for a new boy since you wasn't working and couldn't buy her nothing. No big loss, boy."

Daddy calls 'em like he sees 'em.

♪ ♪ ♪

The last time I'd gone to work, my commute was completely different from this stroll with Daddy.

I was driving a small pickup truck and I'd popped in my current favorite Beatles CD, *Reunion*, because I felt like a little "Liverpool Cowboy." The Lennon/Nelson guitar duo intro and outro were so relaxing that I didn't worry about anything for the whole 5:48. I never would have reckoned a Texas boy like Willie could harmonize with John and Paul, but it worked. Regrettably, it was followed by the Aretha Franklin collaboration that unfortunately did not work at all.

When the CD first came out, a few cynical critics decried it as being gimmicky because there were guest artists on every track except for the hidden track at the end. I was just glad to have a little more music from the band I'd grown up loving, whether good, bad, or mediocre.

While I didn't have my Beatles for company on this commute with Daddy, at least I didn't have to worry about Houston traffic or getting killed by a reckless wrecker driver.

♪ ♪ ♪

Like the 98-pound weakling in gym class, I was the last one picked. My job was to take stuff off the boat and stack it on a wagon. Instead of huge, heavy wooden crates, I lucked out and had to move bags of rough cotton from point A to point B. I sustained scratches from the bags and the stems poking through, but my new hands were still fairly rough, hardly bleeding at all.

After about two hours in the sun, though, I was beginning to slow. While trying to maintain the pace of the other workers, I lost consciousness at least twice but continued working. It's a strange thing to wake up still walking and working after blacking out momentarily. I wanted to stop after passing out the second time, but I assumed that a break would be forthcoming.

At about the three-hour mark, I asked the squat, muscular fellow walking in front of me when we would stop. He stumbled forward as if surprised.

As he turned around, he began, "Well, suh . . .," until he saw me.

Then he barked, "Nigger, don't be scaring a nigger like that, sounding like a White man! You get me put off. That shit ain't funny, nigger."

Huh? I assumed I could pass as Black solely on the basis of my skin color. Lesson learned.

I apologized, trying to sound less White, and his answer was that we would stop when the boss got tired of watching us work.

I never found out exactly how long it took for the boss to get tired of watching us work. Within an hour or so of asking about a break, my body granted me a break by shutting down. I keeled over.

My lower legs turned to rubber, followed by my upper legs and torso. As my body gradually approached the ground, my consciousness started fading, so that by the time I hit the ground, I was unconscious and the impact didn't hurt at all.

I was aware of being moved at least twice, once to be placed atop a couple of bags of cotton, and a second move to an office where I awakened.

A nicely dressed White man sat behind a desk writing in a ledger of some sort. He seemed busy and I felt comfortable where I was, so I allowed myself to lapse into sleep again.

The next time I awakened, the man was seated next to my resting place on a wooden chair with a stuffed seat and back. He smelled nice, like he'd bathed in scented salts and splashed himself with cologne afterwards. I missed baths.

"It's time you awakened," he said softly in a cultured, not-quite British accent.

I looked up at him and thought, *he's cute*, but said, "Okay. Where am I anyway?"

"You're in my office. You fainted while working on the dock."

"Oh, right. Thanks for letting me recover in here. I should be better tomorrow."

He looked me up and down, or perhaps left to right, as I lay on his somewhat worn, but stylish chaise lounge, which matched the chair.

"I don't think you will get much work on the docks for a bit. The dock masters won't forget this episode for some time. Methinks you should consider another line of work."

"To be perfectly honest, I wasn't looking forward to this manual labor thing anyway, but I'm uncertain what other lines of work would be available to me."

He looked at me again, more curiously.

"You look the part, yet don't speak at all like a typical dock worker. In particular, not a Negro dock worker. Who are you?"

Cautiously, I replied, "I'm Matthew Little. And you?"

"I am George Fitzgerald, but I suspect you know that I was not merely asking your name. There are not many, if any, Negroes on the dock to whom manual labor is *infra dig*. Why are you . . . different?"

"Good question, sir. I hate to appear unappreciative after your kindness, but I've got a hunch that you might think me crazy if I give you an honest response. And quite honestly, I'm at a loss for a believable dishonest response."

He chuckled at my avoidance of his query.

"I enjoy a good tale as much as the next gentleman. Tell me yours and I will try not to judge you harshly."

His gray eyes and soft voice seemed sincere, and he really was quite easy on the eyes, so I told him most of my story. George listened politely, hardly raising his eyebrows at the weirder parts.

"You were correct to prelude your tale with a caveat. Yet, I almost believe you. What proof could you offer?"

"I wish that I knew more of the history of this period. I could tell you more about the future in which I lived, and you would be amazed and astounded."

"Do you remember our conversation on the dock just before I had you brought to my office?"

"No. I only recall waking up in here after passing out. Why did you bring me to your office? Is this standard treatment for workers who black out?"

"My reasons were several. Firstly, after you passed out, I went to see what had happened. I asked your name, and you replied, 'Eleanor Ross.' Then I asked if you knew where you were, and you said, 'Houston, Texas, of course.' Finally, I asked you who I am, and you responded, 'I don't know, but I'd like to.' Something in your tone struck me as flirting. Never has any dock worker, Negro or White, flirted with me."

"Oh," I said, slightly embarrassed. "So, now that you know I'm a woman, albeit a woman with a penis, I hope it makes more sense."

"I do not believe that the time has arrived when I can say that a woman with a penis makes sense, but I can say that I accept the fact that *you* sincerely believe this to be true."

Logically, I could not fault his skepticism. To this day, I wonder if this is not the world's longest and most detailed dream. Nevertheless, I felt that since George now knew as much as he did, I should try my gosh-darnedest to convince him.

"Do you have a recent newspaper?" I asked, thinking it might help me to better recall U.S. History 101 from college.

George handed me one from his desk. I scanned the headlines for familiar names and events. The Douglas-Lincoln debates were prominent and I realized then that I at least knew who would be the next President. I relayed to George the fact that Abraham Lincoln would be the next President and he scoffed.

"The likelihood of the log cabin lawyer defeating a man of Mr. Douglas' reputation and stature is minimal. I would even go so far as to wager against the possibility of such an upset."

"If I had any money, I would take your bet. I can't say if Lincoln wins the debates, but he is definitely going to be the next president."

"Then I shall find you a job, young Mr. Little or Miss Whatever, and in due time, your wages shall flow from your hands to mine. But first, see if there is anything else in the newspaper."

"Nothing else rings a bell. Right now, the only other key historical figure I can remember from this time is John Brown. His wave of terror was a major turning point in U.S. history, nearly leading to the dissolution of the Union. Has Brown taken Harper's Ferry yet?"

George sat back in his chair and paused for nearly a minute, pondering what I had just said and looking at me much as Oleta had done, as if puzzling over how much of what I was saying could be believed. I wondered what he saw when looking at my face. I didn't know if this new visage reflected my feelings the same way my old face did. Is mine a face you can trust?

Finally, he said, "Brown's actions in Kansas lead me to believe that what you say is at least a possibility. You are, Mr. Little or Miss Whatever . . ."

"Call me Matthew for now. I've got to get used to it anyway."

"Well then, Matthew. You are, if nothing else, an interesting character and imaginative storyteller. And I think that I would like to get to know you better. The workers will leave soon, so you should leave to wait for your father, but come back tomorrow and I will introduce you to a man who may be able to employ you. I assume that if you were a teacher in your prior life, you are able to write and perform mathematics."

"Yes, I can read, write, add, subtract, multiply, and divide. I'd appreciate anything you can do to help, sir."

"Call me George, when we are alone, but Mr. Fitzgerald elsewhere."

"Understood, George. And thank you."

I extended my hand, which he shook firmly.

"I must be certain you have a means to pay me when your Mr. Lincoln loses. I shan't be penny wise and pound foolish. Good evening, Matthew."

"Good evening to you, George."

I couldn't be certain at the time, but it seemed George was flirting with me a bit too.

♬ ♬ ♬

As we walked home, Daddy only said one thing – "I guess you gonna have to get some inside work now." The word "inside" was pronounced with an understated disdain. Just enough to let me know that "inside" work was not a good thing, but not so much that it showed real emotion. I thought Daddy needed to get in touch with his feminine side, but I wasn't yet man enough to tell him.

I mentioned that Mr. Fitzgerald said he would introduce me to someone who might be willing to hire me, to which Daddy responded, "Umm hmm."

Although I was a police officer for years, I never felt like a man, and harbored no desire to be one. Nonetheless, one thing every female officer has heard is, "So, does that gun make you feel like a man?" followed by some denigratory label ranging from honey, sweetie, little girl, or baby to bitch.

Now that I think about it, I'm reminded of the correlation between assholes who ask female officers if they think they're men and assholes who have outstanding warrants for their arrest. I'd bet ten percent of all of the arrests I ever made were guys who asked me that question.

Today, however, walking home with Daddy, I felt very guy-like. Two working men returning home after a hard day of manual labor, silently reflecting on the day's events and enjoying the beautiful twilight as it reflected off the river's surface. Totally guy-like, right?

Back at home, I gave Oleta a short lesson while Momma looked at me like the proud parent of a newborn. She'd decided I was like Lazarus, but that an angel had seen fit to bestow upon me the additional blessing of literacy.

Neither Daddy nor I felt it necessary to tell her that I'd fainted. No discussion was required.

It's a guy thing.

6

Veni, Vidi, Vici

The following morning I reported directly to George's office, and proceeded to wait about two hours for him to arrive. Understandable. I imagine if I were the owner's son, I wouldn't work the same hours as the manual labor.

Nevertheless, I wished he'd at least had a proper waiting room with a TV to watch or outdated magazines to read. Anything to pass the time.

Instead, I had to sit on a sack of cotton outside his locked door, cogitating and feeling sorry for myself.

As much as I loved movies, I was surprised that I didn't miss television too much, but it would have been nice to have a few good books and a laptop for keeping a diary. And a real toothbrush. And hot and cold

44

running water. And toilet paper. And coffee. And a refrigerator stocked with chocolate ice cream and a variety of good to very good wines.

Sitting on that prickly bag thinking about what I missed didn't make time go by any faster, but it beat working on the dock (except for the lack of pay, of course).

When George finally arrived, I switched into gracious mode, since I was in need of a job and he could help me get one.

"I made a point of getting in early for you, my time traversing friend. I pray you've not had to wait too very long," George announced cheerily as we entered his office.

"Not too long. So you believe my story?"

"I will not allow myself to fully accept your tale, but neither am I willing to discount it. You are definitely more entertaining than my ledger, so our adventure will continue. Follow me."

As George escorted me along the Delaware River, he asked, "Were you truly a female member of the constabulary?"

I smiled, imagining how absurd the notion was to a man of the mid-19th century.

"Yes. I completed all the training, including firearms and hand-to-hand combat. Even boxing."

"Pugilism!" he said, incredulous at the idea of a female boxing.

"It was required."

"The idea of a woman participating in such violent activities boggles the mind. You were a regular Jeanne d'Arc."

"Not quite, but one of my first calls after I was graduated from the police academy was a hostage situation. I didn't get to storm the house with the more experienced guys, but I was in the right place at the right time. The bad guy dove out of a side window right in front of me."

George stopped walking and stared at me.

"What did you do?"

"Well, he landed on his hands and knees with his back to me. Didn't even know I was there. I already had my gun out, so before he had a chance to stand up, I applied my boot to his back and shoved him face first to the ground. Then I put my knee on his spine, and my revolver to the base of his skull. My training officer was next out of the window and he handcuffed the guy."

"Amazing," George said, shaking his head. "A woman besting a man in a physical encounter. Were you afraid?"

"Not until hours later. That's when the reality of it all hit me, but before that, I was just excited. All the guys were clapping me on the back and giving me atta-girls."

"Incredible. Did your family not worry? Did you have a husband and children?"

"No, I never found the right person to marry. And I didn't tell my parents the scary stuff. But as a teacher, I had plenty of children. By the time I got home from a full day in the classroom, I didn't need more kid time."

George took a moment to study me before speaking.

"I think I believe you," he said.

"Really? What convinced you?"

"The things you say are too imaginative, even for a writer of fiction. The way you say them, matter-of-factly, as if they really happened. And clearly your speech pattern is not of this, nor of any other place with which I am familiar. I am of the belief that most things, especially momentous things such as a journey through time, happen for a reason."

Then he asked me essentially the exact question Oleta had.

"So, Matthew, why have you traveled here, now?"

Again, I had no answer. But George's belief in my story comforted me, and made me feel more sane and less completely alone.

We continued walking over the equivalent of several city blocks before stopping in front of a fairly small office connected to a larger warehouse.

As we approached the office, through the glass I saw a serious-looking Black man comparing the contents of two books. When we turned toward the door, however, he seemed to be poring over a single ledger.

I notice little things like that. Probably a throwback to my police career, but it came in handy as a teacher too. The kids almost believed me when I told them I had eyes in the back of my head.

Anyway, when I notice little things like that, I go on alert and consciously watch for other suspicious activities and signs of danger to myself and/or others.

"*Salve, bone vir!*" George bellowed with a wide grin to the Black man as he opened the door.

"*Salve tantundem mihi, carissime!*" the Black man roared back, grinning equally broadly. "*Quid me vis?*"

I later learned that the two men always greeted each other in Latin. George explained that they merely said *good day* to each other and *what brings you to me?*

"Matthew," George said to me, "I would like to introduce to you Mr. William Still. Mr. Still owns this office and assists me in making certain that the dead language of Latin survives, albeit in gravely ill health."

"Good to meet you, sir," I said, offering my hand.

"William, I would like to introduce to you Matthew Little, a young man in need of employment," George said as Still eyed me suspiciously while shaking my hand.

"As you know, George, I generally hire my labor through the dock pool as you do."

"Actually, this young man requires indoor work, as his health is yet poor since recovering from the plague or some other such ailment."

Still looked me up and down. No trace of the smile he gave George was shared with me.

"You know I work alone," he stated seriously to George, as if I weren't there.

George nodded and then glanced at me before responding. Clearly, the Black businessman had secrets, and strong reservations about hiring anyone who might uncover them.

"There is more to young Matthew than his appearance would lead you to believe. *Peream, si mentiar!*" [translation: The devil take me if I lie.]

"If my cargo is in any way harmed by his presence, you will have more to fear than the devil. My work is neither a game nor a craft to which one can take an apprentice, George."

"As a favor to me, just talk with him, please. I will make him presentable if you were to give him a chance."

I should explain why Still was so concerned just from looking at me. My wardrobe in full consisted of three pairs of pants and three shirts, all of which appeared to be older than the body I inhabited. Between the holes and the stains, I looked more like an escapee from debtor's prison than a young man on a job interview. I suppose Still could only see a dockworker since I was in dockworker's garb.

He, on the other hand, was a distinguished gentleman with his hair parted on the left, wearing polished shoes, a dark suit, white shirt, and some sort of bowtie. Compared to him, I looked homeless.

After nearly a minute of silence while Still considered my fate, I spoke up.

"I, too, would hesitate to hire me Mr. Still, considering my appearance, even on the referral of a good friend. One can say that all men are equal and one shouldn't judge a book by its cover, but in business matters, one must be practical. I freely submit myself to whatever pre-employment tests you wish to utilize. If I fail, I promise not to file suit on the basis of discrimination."

George smirked while Still looked at me in much the same way that Oleta and George did after I first spoke to them. Then he gave me a sheet of paper and a pencil, and asked me to add several series of numbers. Then he gave me word problems dealing with counting and basic accounting matters. Finally, he gave me a spelling test.

After nearly an hour of testing and questions about my political beliefs (including whether I was for Douglas or Lincoln), Still gave me a small smile and asked that I report to work that afternoon after I purchased proper clothing and footwear, and did something with my hair.

Another word of explanation is in order here. Black hair is different from White hair. Very different. I tried water like I did with Oleta's hair, but it hurt too much to comb through Matthew's hair. Most days, I combed a bit at the front and left it at that. My thinking was that I

50

was not out to impress anyone anyway. As the days passed, it became easier for me to comb more and more of the hair on top of my head, but I could find no compelling reason to punish myself by trying to untangle the mess on the tender sides and back of my scalp. Until now.

George loaned me the money for new clothes and directed me to the proper store.

That was the easy part.

Next, I went home to work on my hair. Oleta jokingly advised me to cut it off and start over. From the mouths of babes.

She walked me to the Negro barber and stayed to mock me. I guess that's what little sisters are for.

By the way, I say Negro barber because Negro is the preferred term of the more genteel. I've had to remind myself to use that term to avoid attracting attention.

Even a very short haircut required some use of the comb by the barber, and I will now confess to shedding a tear or two from the pain. Nobody asked, but I was prepared to tell them that the tears were from the tiny hairs irritating my eyes. Daddy would have been proud.

The barber must have known Matthew and tried to start a conversation. After I spoke for the first time though, he looked at me like Oleta, George, and William Still had. Then he silently finished my hair in a businesslike manner.

I was gathering that I would need to learn to speak differently in order to fit in within certain circles.

ℰ ℰ ℰ

I returned to William Still a new man, so to speak.

The question of my salary had not yet been broached, so I broached. Still simply replied that my hiring was on a trial basis, and assured me I would, without question, make more than I would standing around the docks *not* getting chosen for one of the work crews.

My first job was to sweep the cavernous warehouse and office area. Still did not know my entire story, so he had no idea that I possessed a college degree (not to mention a knowledge of the future, and phantom breasts – I kept thinking they were there). Therefore, I could not complain that I was overqualified for the task. Compared to hauling sacks of cotton, this was the sweet life, *la dolce vita*.

When I finished, if one can ever truly finish sweeping a working warehouse, Still gave me paper and a pencil.

"I need a count on everything unloaded by the North Wind today. Should be the tobacco in the far corner. Count at least twice. Mistakes come out of your pay," Still said dryly.

"Yes sir," I responded, and he nodded in acknowledgment. It seemed that I was doing better at making friends with a White man than with Blacks. Still was as cold as I would have expected a White boss to act toward me.

During my old life, I'd had Black friends.

In high school, Eliot played football and ran track, while I played volleyball and basketball. Half the athletes on any team at our school were Black, except for baseball for some reason. Sports have always had a social component, so you learned to work together in order to win. Color didn't matter – a teammate was a teammate, both on and off the field.

After I became a teacher, I found that one of Eliot's best friends from high school, who was Black, was in charge of the computer lab at my school. Randon had run track with Eliot, but had also been editor of the high school newspaper. We recognized each other at a summer teachers' meeting and became good work friends.

Randon helped me with my weekly tech problems, but more importantly, he and his wife helped me cope with Eliot's death. They checked in with me every day, dropped off food, and sat beside me at the funeral service. Good people.

Yet somehow here in 1858, as an actual Black person (albeit in skin only), I struggled to fit in. Something else I'd have to work on.

Counting tobacco bundles is trickier than it might sound and it occupied the rest of my short day. The stacks were uneven so I wound up moving bundles in order to count the back row. As I replaced the bundles, I made the stacks even to facilitate my second count.

Still nodded when I gave him the figures and told me he'd see me in the morning.

ℰ ℰ ℰ

Daddy had nearly another hour to work, judging by the amount of light in the sky, so I stopped by George's office to give him a progress report.

"William is a very serious man most of the time," George reassured me. "It's nothing personal. He has a tremendous amount of responsibility and takes nothing lightly, as you will see. In time he will warm to you. How's your Latin?"

"Tempus fugit. E pluribus unum. Id est. Exempli gratia. A la carte. Corpus Delecti. Veni, vidi, vici. Carpe diem."

"I see. William has a thing for learning Latin, so you might brush up a bit. And, by the way, *a la carte* is French."

"I lack the means to brush up, i.e. textbooks, but moreover, I never studied Latin."

"Is Latin not required in public school nor universities in your time?"

"Not at all required. In most places, it isn't even offered as an elective."

"What languages have you studied?"

"A little Spanish. It seemed the most sensible in Texas."

"The fact that you are a Texican is almost as odd as the entire time displacement matter. Your voice sounds nothing of the South. How is that?"

I spent the next 45 minutes until Daddy got off work explaining television and the things that led up to television such as radio, motion pictures, and electricity. He was especially surprised that Benjamin Franklin's kite experiment of over 100 years before had led to so much.

"I shall watch for matters utilizing this electricity on the stock exchange and perhaps make my fortune. If this works out in any way, I shall not forget you, my friend," George remarked.

Now it was my turn to be surprised. "There's a stock exchange in 1858?"

"Since the latter part of the last century," George answered.

As I left him, I began wondering if I was becoming the first inside trader. Also, was I altering history in any discernible way? My working theory was that what has happened, has happened and my actions, if anything, led to and are part of the future from which I came.

But as jazzman Fats Waller once said, "One never knows, do one?"

$$\delta \quad \delta \quad \delta$$

Daddy took the news of my new job with his usual enthusiasm – none. He did mumble a "yup" when I mentioned having to restack the tobacco.

I interpreted that to mean, "I'm quite proud of you for getting a job so quickly and for acquitting yourself so admirably on your first day," but I suppose I could be off by a word or two. I was not yet fluent in guy-speak.

Momma, on the other hand, gushed and praised my job and new outfit, going so far as to speculate that Mr. William Still might give me his job when he sees fit to stop working. Apparently, Still was a big deal in the Black community.

Matters of hygiene were among the most trying adjustments to living in this time. I could not take a shower at all, and full baths were a once-a-week occurrence. At age sixteen, I was young enough that facial hair was not a problem, but my underarm hair imbued me with an odor only a canine could love by Fridays. My one work outfit could only be cleaned once per week until I could afford to purchase a second outfit. Dental floss was simply not there. Four out of five dentists definitely did *not* recommend my toothbrush and toothpaste.

But one gets used to the feeling of never being squeaky clean and never smelling April fresh, and then one goes on with life.

During my second week of employment, as George predicted, William Still began to warm to me as we spoke of things other than work. I told him about Oleta and my desire to find a school for her. Education was a topic dear to him, and at the mention of it, I saw his estimation of me increase by at least 50%. His first question was why did I not send her to the school that I'd attended.

Given the choice of telling the full story to another person or lying, I chose the simpler course of prevarication. My explanation that I was self-taught was accepted, if not totally believed. My ignorance of Latin made the self-taught line somewhat believable, but my speech pattern always seemed to cast suspicion on my statements.

"If admission could be gained," Still began, "Mrs. Henry Gordon's private school and the Friends Raspberry Alley School are excellent, and might offer financial assistance of a sort. My Caroline has attended both, but there is also a public Negro school that may have room for young Oleta. And when she is older, the Institute for Colored Youth is recommended."

He wrote down the information for me and even offered to pen a letter of recommendation. Just like in my time, concern for children can sometimes bring people together.

I remember when President Richards selected actor LeVar Burton as Secretary of Education. She took a lot of flak for appointing the Reading Rainbow guy to the post. She stuck to her guns though, and he won people over with a combination of charm, passion, and his fundraising ability.

Who knew the guy had a PhD in Education? Secretary Burton immediately began innovating and working toward a national curriculum, wisely going one subject at a time, beginning with math.

Congress was initially resistant, but once former presidents Kennedy, Anderson, and Reagan, along with their spouses, came aboard, all three political parties came around and the program was off and running. Even Vice President Takei and former VP Bush, who never agreed on anything, jumped on the bandwagon.

Burton wisely hired retired and experienced teachers as advisors, both to craft the curriculum and to aid in developing software to assist with teaching concepts and assessing progress. Before I died, I was looking forward to letting computers do the bulk of the work and just acting as a facilitator and remediator.

♪ ♪ ♪

During my third week with Still, I discovered the reason for his sober demeanor. While looking for the ledger to enter inventory data, I accidentally picked up the wrong ledger. It was the second ledger that had so suddenly disappeared when I first saw Still through the window.

I had never seen it left out before and was reading it before I realized it was not the regular book. To snoop or not to snoop. Silly question.

In a matter of seconds, it was obvious that some arriving shipments were not being recorded in the primary ledger. Further, some outgoing shipments were larger in the second ledger than in the primary book.

This indicated that Still was either stealing or smuggling items along with regular shipments. Neither possibility struck me as consistent with what I'd observed of Still's character until I considered the obvious. It was 1858 with slavery still in full bloom. Perhaps the additional items were related to aiding and abetting escaped slaves. Good for him!

I replaced the second ledger and would have respected Still's privacy but for the arrival of a crate soon thereafter containing an unscheduled and wholly unexpected cargo.

Still said he was not expecting the crate, and, since there was no forwarding address, he ordered me to open it and let him know what it held. The box was pretty much a cube, measuring about four feet on each side. It was constructed of the same type of splintery wood used for pallets in the 1990s.

I wheeled the crate closer to the office on a handcart so I wouldn't have to carry its contents too far for delivery. Then I wedged a lever between the box and its nailed-on cover and pressed downward. Next I pried the opposite corner of the box and did the same to the other corners. As I removed the cover, I got a large splinter in my right ring finger, so I placed the cover on the ground, muttered a mild oath, and proceeded to doctor my digit.

While extracting the wood from my finger, I thought I heard a sound coming from the box, like a throat clearing. I paused a second to listen.

Nothing.

When I was done with the splinter, I shifted my attentions back to the crate. Inside it, I observed a sweaty, filthy, and not surprisingly, remarkably odoriferous Black male who looked to be in his early 30s. He was scrunched and folded upon himself, staring up at me. We looked at each other for fifteen or twenty seconds without speaking.

Finally, I snapped to what was happening, and smiled, saying, "Welcome to Philadelphia, Pennsylvania, sir."

He smiled back nervously, asking, "Is it safe?"

"Yes. No one is here except us."

"I'm sho glad I saw you before I heard you talk, boy. I ain't know niggers talk like White folk up north. You like to scared me to death. I mighta died thinking I was still a slave."

"Actually, my speech patterns are different from most. That is, Negroes here speak, well, some speak more like me, and some speak more like you, and some speak kind of in between."

"You one fancy-talking nigger."

"Thank you, I think. Stay right here while I get Mr. Still. He'll know what to do with you."

The man's eyes got large with fear. He obviously assumed Still was White.

"Don't worry. Mr. Still is a Negro and knows how to help. We'll get you taken care of."

"Would you mind helping me out this here box first? I ain't sho I can take another minute all squoze up in here."

I used the lever to remove another side of the box to facilitate the man's exit. Unable to stand and stiff from his confinement, he rolled out onto the warehouse floor.

"Sorry," I said. "I guess I didn't think that through."

He just looked at me and began chuckling.

"Me neither, boy," he said, still laughing, "but rolling 'round here on the floor still beat picking cotton any day."

I laughed with him and bent down to begin massaging his back, arms, and legs. Shortly, he could sit and then, with some effort, stand.

When he was sufficiently loosened up, we sauntered into the front office area. I said to Still with a grin, "I present to you the contents of the crate you asked me to open."

Still looked up from his desk, turned, made eye contact with the man and then me, and sighed.

"Who sent you?" he asked the man.

"Me."

"Yes, you, who sent you?"

"Me, suh, I sent me."

"And who are you?" Still asked humorlessly, despite the smiles on my face and that of the box man.

"My name is Toby Green, suh. From —"

"Well, welcome to Philadelphia, Mr. Green, and to freedom."

From that moment on, I became Still's associate in slave smuggling. Shipments arrived intermittently, though not in crates like Toby, and we kept them until members of the Philadelphia Vigilance Society picked them up.

Still kept another book in which he logged the arriving shipments' stories of their escapes. I told him it might be interesting to publish it upon the abolition of slavery, to which he replied that he only hoped to live that long.

Of course, I knew that slavery would begin to be phased out during Lincoln's administration, but since it would not completely end until the turn of the century, I kept that bit of knowledge to myself. The Emancipation Compromise nearly cost Lincoln his second term in office and brought the country to the brink of an internal war that could have ended the nation.

Although Blacks in Philadelphia were free, ostensibly with all the rights of Whites, a social order existed wherein Blacks knew their place. Certain neighborhoods and establishments were off limits, as well as certain jobs. I suppose the segregation was in part economic, but it was clear that even dirt poor Whites were above most Blacks in status.

As bad as it was to be Black in 1858 in Philly, I could only imagine how much worse it was in the South.

7

The Elephant in the Room (or Veni, pt. II)

I have not spoken much of my home life because there was not much of a home life. I worked six days a week for ten to twelve hours per day. When I got home, I ate, had a short lesson with Oleta, cleaned myself as best I could, and collapsed.

Sundays, I was supposed to go to church, but I avoided it by pleading fatigue. Since Matthew had already died once, Momma and Daddy cut me some slack.

Once everyone else left for church, I slept for another hour or so. Then I cleaned up, dressed, and left to wander the city.

Well, actually, that's not all I did.

Okay. I know I should be embarrassed to write about this, but scientists might find it interesting, and, let's face it – I'll have been dead a very long time before anyone reads it.

What's among the first things you'd do if you were a gal who found herself occupying a guy's body, or vice versa?

Naturally, as soon as I found a private moment, I found my privates.

It's what any gal who'd had her essence transferred into the body of a man would do, I'm sure. I'm quite certain any guy would do the same if he found himself to be a woman.

Fascinating stuff, male physiology.

So weird. One minute it's just hanging there, asleep or dormant or whatever. Next thing you know, it's alive and demanding attention.

Plainly, I'm a show-er and a grower. As Madeline Kahn so eloquently voiced in *Blazing Saddles,* "It's twue, it's twue!"

This was not my first penis, but it was my first Black penis, and certainly the first to which I've been physically attached. And it's definitely the first which I've had time to examine at length, so to speak.

The first thing that jumped out at me was that it was much darker than the rest of my skin when flaccid, but once erect, while still darker, it matched up better.

I was uncircumcised, which I quickly determined meant it required daily cleaning to avoid a sharp smell. That also meant the head was far more sensitive to the touch than I would have imagined.

I'd always been curious about why guys reacted so strongly when their testicles were struck. A quick flick to one of them with my index finger told me all I cared to know.

♂ ♂ ♂

The whole penis thing took considerable getting used to. Perhaps because of Matthew's age at the time, it was particularly responsive.

Every morning, without fail, *it* stood at attention. I suppose that was *its* way of saying, "Good morning, at your service!"

Not knowing how long I'd be here, I wanted the full experience.

Was there a physiological imperative that I act upon this? I don't think so. Not that it mattered because I was as curious as a child at Christmas.

What should I do?

Okay, that was easy. The "when" was more complicated.

Privacy was at a premium, with five people sharing a total of three small rooms. Sundays were best, and on my third Sunday there, I was left completely alone for the first time.

As my twin brother Eliot said after seeing *The Rocky Horror Picture Show* for the first and only time, "Now that's some weird shit."

Anyway, I came to love Sundays. Considering how little training I've had, I quickly became quite proficient with this thing. The experience was not as full bodied as when I was female, and far messier, but was nonetheless addictive.

♂ ♂ ♂

Initially, the sensation of the morning erection wasn't sexual.

However, I began to have strange dreams in which I as Matthew made love to me as Eleanor. At first, I, as Matthew, was a student in my class, despite Matthew's age. Sometimes, I, as Eleanor, seduced Matthew. Sometimes, I, as Matthew, seduced Eleanor.

Sometimes, though, the dreams got really weird.

Despite being 41 years old at the time of my death, I hadn't been with very many men. I like to believe that was by choice.

Only in my last few years as a female had I begun to get past my upbringing and realize that I didn't find men particularly sexy.

Sure, some men are attractive, some are funny, and some are interesting, but none really got me worked up. Once I came to that realization and accepted that it was not deviant to feel that way, I began to ask myself the obvious question.

At the beginning of the current school year, a new art teacher, Abby, arrived. We were paired off in a getting to know each other exercise during one of our classroom preparation days prior to the start of the school year and the conversation just flowed. The silly things like favorite colors, music, and foods seemed significant because we shared them. It was just a natural friendship.

For a few weeks, we were just work friends, having lunch together and chatting after school. Then we hit upon a passion we couldn't share at work – bowling.

During the summer between our sophomore and junior years in high school, Eliot and I decided that we would practice early every Sunday morning at Bellaire Lanes until we became good enough to become pro bowlers. We never averaged much over 160, but we each broke 200 a couple of times and had fun with our fantasy.

Bellaire Lanes was still open over thirty years later.

Abby had been married before but had no children. She did, however, have her own ball and shoes.

Our competition was good-natured and we'd cheer for each other, high fiving and high tenning. On our last outing before my death, I needed a strike in the ninth frame to have any chance at breaking 150.

I knew when the ball left my hand, I had my strike. Smiling, I turned to Abby and she strode over to give me a full-on bear hug.

Embarrassed, I pulled away quicker than either of us wanted to. She laughed it off, punching me lightly on the shoulder.

Later, at dinner, our knees touched under the table.

Neither of us pulled away.

I felt like a high schooler on a first date, giddy and nervous.

That's when I knew for certain that we both wanted to be more than friends and it was just a matter of time before something more would happen. Only now, nothing will ever happen with Abby. Except in my weird dreams.

Death sucks.

♂ ♂ ♂

The testosterone effect on the brain is real. With my new experiences, I finally began to understand why men often ignore common sense.

I'd never had a high sex drive as a woman, except for the first few months after I discovered my magic button.

As a man, I felt compelled to masturbate. My head said no, but my other head said yes, yes, yesssss.

Maybe I'm oversharing, but ideally, I'll get this document in the future and get a good laugh out of it.

I really do hope I get this document in the future and I'll avoid all of this bizarreness, including the mess I was about to get into.

8

I Meet Harriet Tubman

William Still and I never became close friends, although we had a good working relationship and shared several excellent conversations about the future of the Negro in America. I suspected that for all his concern about the poor Negro slaves, he, to some extent, could not wholly relate to poor Negro freemen.

However, after I had been privy to his sideline enterprise for several months, he invited me to a meeting of the Philadelphia Vigilance Committee. It was early spring of 1859 and Harriet Tubman was scheduled to speak. After months of relative mundanity, I would finally get to witness history.

I didn't recall exactly when, but I knew that Harriet Tubman was caught and hanged for smuggling slaves out of the South in the fall of 1859. It was a major turning point in history because it fueled the fires of the abolition movement. Hanging a woman enraged seemingly everyone in the North, driving huge numbers to speak out and take action.

In the South, every Black person (and some Whites) recognized that the status quo could not last with the rising tension, unrest, and outright anger of both abolitionists and the enslaved.

Knowing that Tubman would be dead soon meant I would be hearing one of her last public speeches.

If anyone else knew what I knew, tickets for this would go faster than the '86 Beatles reunion concert. I missed the live show, but caught it on pay-per-view. Not a bad show for a former skiffle band.

Anyway, Still and I met up with our mutual friend George at the Vigilance Hall. Attendees were mainly White and male, with the race ratio probably proportional to the city's population. Women were fewer in attendance, as would be expected in this era, but those who were there had enough spirit to make up for the lack of numbers. These were the bleeding heart liberals of the time.

Just as before any event, small groups chatted amongst themselves about current happenings. More than one group got worked up over the Dred Scott decision by the Supreme Court in the previous year.

Scott was a slave who'd sued for his freedom based on the fact that his master had transported him into states that outlawed slavery. Some were more outraged about the court deciding that Scott was mere property, the loss of which the so-called owner would suffer if freedom were granted. Others were angrier that the court pronounced that no person of African descent could claim U.S. citizenship.

One young woman, who introduced herself as Victoria Claflin Woodhull, spoke before Tubman. As she concluded her brief remarks, she asked Tubman if she would be her running mate when she ran for president in a few years. Most of the men got a good laugh out of that, but Tubman flashed only the tiniest of grins and, after the laughter quieted, responded thoughtfully, "I'll think on it, Miss."

The man introducing Tubman spent several minutes describing her as "a heroine and storyteller nonpareil," and advising us to "prepare to be astounded, amused, and thoroughly entertained." When he finally called her to speak, though, he called her Harriet Garrison, I suppose to avoid exposing her true identity to any spies that might be present.

As the applause died down following the introduction, the short, muscular, dark-skinned Tubman looked up to the ceiling and began singing in a low, resonant voice:

When Israel was in Egypt's land,
Let my people go.
Oppress'd so hard they could not stand,
Let my People go.
Go down, Moses,
Way down in Egypt's land,
Tell old Pharaoh,
Let my people go.

"I growed up hating White folk," she began with a broad grin, "and now here I is in a room full of y'all."

Laughter.

"Now," she continued, gesturing with her large hands, "after getting helped to freedom by a nice Quaker woman and man, now I is proud to say Colored and White can work together. Now I is proud to call you all friends."

Thunderous applause and nods of agreement.

From that moment on, she had us eating out of her hands.

Most of Tubman's talk consisted of stories about her life as a slave and her life as Moses, her nickname because she too led her people out of bondage. The audience sat rapt as she spoke, and probably could have asked questions all night had Still and James McKim, a preacher of some sort, not escorted her away.

I wanted to talk to her, but I felt unworthy. Starstruck at my age, if you can imagine.

ଫ ଫ ଫ

To my surprise and pleasure, Tubman dropped in to visit Still the following evening at work. He asked me to tell her the story about Toby "Box" Green, as we had taken to calling him. Fortunately, I had practiced telling the story to Oleta and George, so I performed the story as much as I told it, folding my body as Toby's was in the box, and struggling to stand after being restricted in tight quarters for over 24 hours.

The tiny woman gave me a large smile when I finished. I believe I would have blushed had I been the me that I once was. Maybe I still blushed, albeit less visibly.

As I went back to work, I overheard her tell Still, "He talk even more like a White man than you."

She was just departing as I was leaving work. I wanted to walk with her a while, but didn't want to bother her. After we had proceeded about a block, she said, without looking around, "Walk with me a bit, boy."

"Thank you."

"You act like I'm a massuh or something. I'm just Harriet."

"Thank you," I said again. She was my first celebrity, my first brush with greatness, so naturally my conversational skills chose to abandon me.

"Well, I guess you welcome then, boy."

I was still not fully used to the boy, man, Black, penis thing, so every time someone referred to me by sex or race, I took a half-step longer than normal to recognize they were talking to me. Harriet noticed my hesitation and looked at me with her bright eyes much like Oleta did, head tilt and all.

We walked together for only a couple of blocks before I had to turn onto our street. I wished I could have warned her about her future, but all the time travel stories and movies warn about altering the space-time continuum, so I figured I'd better keep my silence.

ℰ ℰ ℰ

The next morning was Saturday, so I decided to walk about town a bit and perhaps do a little shopping. With my salary, after paying my portion of the rent, a very little shopping was definitely all I could do.

Harriet was out walking at the same time so I decided to follow her a ways. I couldn't say exactly what my motivation was. I knew I wouldn't tell her of her fate, but I was curious about her. Her clothing was shabbier than yesterday and seemed to be layered, as if it were cooler than it was, and she set a brisk pace. After following for about thirty minutes or more, I realized we were heading out of Philadelphia. South out of Philadelphia.

Yankee geography never really meant much to me until after I died. I was a Houston girl, born and bred. I memorized data about northern states for tests, but didn't retain the info in long-term memory.

When the Oilers won the Super Bowl with Earl Campbell in '79, the whole city united and it felt like we were just one big family. Mom, Dad, Eliot, and I couldn't wipe the silly grins off of our faces after that game.

And I couldn't have been prouder when the Rockets won their string of championships in the nineties. The titles over New York and Orlando were sweet, but the back-to-back wins over Chicago were especially thrilling. Pippen and Kerr were so great that I almost felt a little sad for them. The Bulls were likely one player away from a dynasty.

By the end of the nineties, after the Comets were WNBA champs for three years running, Houston felt like the center of the sports universe. We were just waiting for the Astros to finally get to the World Series.

What I'm saying is that my world was Texas. The states up north never interested me much. Compared to Texas, they were so small and there were so many of them that I never paid much attention to their locations until this crazy thing happened to me.

Thanks to my new circumstances, common sense dictated I be more geographically aware. The simple fact was that Pennsylvania is darned close to Maryland, a slave state, and therefore a location hazardous to my health. I was already a little lost, so I had to make a decision.

Should I click my heels together three times and hope to get home that way? Should I call out to Harriet and ask how to get home? Or should I utilize these newly acquired cajones of mine and embark upon the adventure of a lifetime, continuing to follow Harriet Tubman on one of her last trips to free slaves?

Hmmm?

Well, the heel-clicking thing didn't work, and I guess the Y chromosome, don't-ask-for-directions-at-any-cost gene was strong within me as Matthew. Oh boy, as the guy on "Quantum Leap" would say.

♂ ♂ ♂

The hot book of the times was *Uncle Tom's Cabin* by Harriet Beecher Stowe. George had loaned me a copy, so I had some idea what to expect if I actually found myself in the South. At the very least, I knew enough to expect surprises.

While following Harriet Tubman, I wondered if she would object to company. Based on what I'd read and heard about her, she worked alone.

After another thirty minutes or so, I lost sight of her somehow. I stopped in a panic. Then, from behind me, I heard a familiar voice say, "Walk with me a bit, boy."

"Thank you," I replied, and that's all it took for us to come to travel together.

We walked in silence for as long as I could stand it. Finally, after about fifteen minutes, I asked her if there was a plan and how could I help.

Her only response was, "We'll see."

I really wanted to phone home to let everyone know where I was, but I'd apparently left my cellular in the other timeline. Hopefully they'd understand. Hopefully I'd return.

♪ ♪ ♪

We slept out in the open all night on the good side (for those of us of the Negro persuasion) of the Mason-Dixon line. Dinner was just fruit and jerky. Bedding was foliage. After walking all day, though, I had no problem sleeping.

As we entered Delaware early the next morning, I expected to skulk about in the woods, but Harriet walked down the main road, making no attempt to hide when approached by Whites. Few people stopped us, possibly because we were walking south and in no particular hurry.

When we were stopped, Harriet simply said we were hired out for day work. As she spoke, one of her hands was always in her cloak on her pistol.

"Why do you risk your life this way?" I asked.

"You ain't never been a slave, has you boy? If you had, you wouldn't ask why."

I nodded to acknowledge my ignorance.

"The Lord chose me to help. He watch over me and keep me from harm as long as I do His will."

At some point during every school year, a student would somehow find out I'd been a police officer. When word got around, without fail, a child would ask if I'd ever shot anyone. My standard reply was a cryptic, "That's not an appropriate topic for the classroom."

I had a similar question for Harriet, but didn't want to sound like a fangirl. As her travelling companion, however, I needed to know in case we got into a dicey situation.

"Would you really use your gun on a runaway who tried to go back, like you said in your talk the other night?"

Harriet chuckled a moment, but then turned serious. "I ain't had to yet, cause most folk figure anybody crazy enough to come back South after being free is crazy enough to do whatever they say they gone do. But, if a patrol or one of my passengers gone do something that gone get me caught, then yep, I will do whatever I gots to to stop 'em. See boy, I ain't never gone be a slave again."

Then Harriet asked with a grin, "Have anybody ever tole you that you sound mo' like a rich White man than a po' Black boy?"

I smiled back at her and said, "Yes indeed, a few people have."

9

Bodhisattva (or Golden Slumbers)

During the afternoon of the second day on the road, Harriet did a most peculiar thing. It changed my life greatly, and, in retrospect, changed her life as I knew it.

She lay down in the grass beside the road and went to sleep. This was no catnap, but a dead-to-the-world, REM sleep from which she could not be roused.

Trust me, I tried.

I mean, at first, for maybe five minutes, I just stood there watching her dumbly. Then, I sat down for another five minutes or so, watching just as dumbly, but from a different (seated) perspective. Finally, after two men in a wagon stopped to ask what we niggers were doing – I replied, "We is going to do some day work, suh" – I felt I should awaken Harriet.

I whispered, spoke loudly, shouted, shook, tickled, and dragged, but she would not stir. Plainly, she was alive, but she did not react.

A horrible thought struck me. What if this is the time when Harriet is caught and hung? What if history now shows that Harriet *and* an accomplice are caught and hung by the neck until dead? Oh, shit!

I dragged Harriet farther off the road and renewed my attempts to rouse her. No luck, so I dragged her into the brush, far enough away from the road that she could not be seen. Then I did the only other thing I could think to do – I sat next to her and waited for her to wake up.

My imagination shifted into overdrive. I envisioned everything from both of us getting caught and hung, to being declared a hero for saving Harriet Tubman from capture.

The sun couldn't go down quickly enough for me. And it didn't.

Just as the sun touched the horizon, I began to hear what sounded like dogs barking in the distance. The distance was distant enough that I figured they weren't looking for us, but the possibility always existed that they could stumble across us. Questions would be asked to which I had no answer, or even a good bluff.

I redoubled my efforts to awaken Harriet to no avail. Finally, I began covering her with damp leaves, all the while trying to decide if I should try to save myself since she was supposed to die anyway, or save her at risk to myself (although technically, I had already died too).

Saving her would be more than a butterfly flapping its wings and causing a minor ripple in time. Was this why I was here in 1859? To save Harriet Tubman? Perhaps I had already saved her in my future and this was always my role.

My saving her could mean she would free someone who in turn became the great grandparent of the person who created the panacea for all kinds of cancer. Or she could free someone who became the grandparent of the person who caused the car wreck that killed the person who would have cured cancer.

I had no way to know or logically determine the best course of action.

By default, I opted to save Harriet.

I say default because while I was trying to reason out the best course of action, the barking had became more frenzied and purposeful, and probably too close for me to get away anyway. My choice became to either save her in the hope that she would rescue me later, or to allow us both to be captured.

I headed toward the sounds until I could see movement in the undergrowth ahead. Knowing the dogs would follow, I began running in the direction I believed to be north. Having never speed tested this body, I had no idea whether I was fast or slow or somewhere in-between.

I began awkwardly, but soon found a rhythm. The running felt so good that I decided to open the throttle completely and give freedom a chance. I could tell the gap between the dogs and me was widening as their yelps began fading. For a brief interval, I hoped against hope that I would get away.

Suddenly, one of the hounds let loose a bloodcurdling howl, and the urgent yaps of the pack again closed in on me. The dogs had apparently been unleashed. Trying not to panic, I continued quickly but carefully to avoid tripping as the classic female victim does in the movies. My new goal became any tree that I could swiftly scramble up to escape the jaws of the canine squad.

Why'd they have to use dogs anyway? Dogs are just plain rude. They're scent junkies. Without so much as a pardon moi, they sniff you in places no one should be sniffed.

Plus, those buggers sounded big – big barks and big bodies crashing over the undergrowth and through the bushes.

They coulda used cats. Cats woulda sniffed me out just fine, only on their own schedule. And more quietly, with smaller teeth.

Enough light filtered through the forest canopy for me to spy a decent climbing tree about fifty yards ahead.

The hounds sounded like they were about half that distance behind. I shifted into overdrive, reaching the tree a good five yards ahead of my pursuers. Fear transformed me into Sheena of the Jungle, as I pulled myself smoothly into the lower branches of the tree.

Not bad for a woman who had to stay after classes every day of the police academy because she couldn't climb the rope in P.T. (physical training).

As I looked down at some other man's best friends, I realized that my lungs had caught fire from my jog. The thought crossed my mind that this would be a good time to wake up, if this were a nightmare.

"Yah, yah, boys!" a rough voice shouted from the now dimly lit path that I had just blazed.

A shortish, red-faced, redheaded White male emerged, followed by an equally short, ginger-haired teen. Only one of the pair had a gun. Were it not for the three dogs, I might have been able to disarm him.

"Down, nigger!" ordered Old Red.

"Yah, down nigger!" echoed Young Red.

"I'm not a slave," I wheezed, trying to catch my breath. "I got lost. I'm from Philadelphia, Pennsylvania."

"Down, nigger! Now!"

"Okay, as soon as the dogs are restrained." Damned mutts!

The boy gathered the frenzied hounds and whispered something to his father.

"I don't care how he talks. He's a nigger, and niggers mean money, boy. Other folk can worry about his story."

I carefully descended from my perch, regaining my wind and watchful for any opportunity to escape. Old Red kept his rifle pointed at me, directing the boy to use his rope to tie my hands and hobble my legs, both to each other and to my arms. Now that the dogs were calmer, I forced my fear to a back burner. I didn't know how far we might be traveling or if Harriet had awakened, so I had to be ready to extricate myself.

A slow march took us near to where I had left Harriet, but only one of the dogs, a massive black and tan bloodhound with a steady stream of drool flowing from his fleshy jowls, seemed to notice. The two other mutts remained focused on returning home, so the odd dog out was ignored.

A short time later, we reached the Reds' wagon. I was tired and sweaty, and brightened at the prospect of riding a bit. Instead, the gol-durned dogs were loaded onto the wagon bed and Old Red tethered me to the rear.

The boy drove the single mule-drawn vehicle while the man sat with the mongrels, dispassionately watching me trot behind. Fortunately, Young Red did not set too swift a pace and the weather was mild.

In less than an hour, we arrived at what I assumed to be a plantation. We stopped outside a moderately

84

impressive house constructed of stone and wood. An oversized barn was nearby with a cluster of smaller shacks visible roughly fifty yards away. On the whole, though, it was no Tara. Furrowed fields with green sprouts were visible beyond the shacks, but in the late evening light I couldn't tell what the cash crop was.

Since plantations usually grow cotton, if Harriet didn't rescue me soon, I could become a cotton picker for true.

Then a barrage of thoughts assailed me at once. What if Harriet was seriously ill and never awakened? What if a bear got her? What if this is really not a dream and I can't convince whomever that I'm a free person? The only thing I didn't imagine was what occurred next.

The door to the main house opened, and a tall, somewhat distinguished looking man of about fifty exited. He and Old Red huddled for about five minutes before he returned to the house and gave Old Red what appeared to be money. The men beckoned Young Red over and then sent him to one of the small cabins.

Red the younger returned with a medium-sized, dark-haired man of perhaps forty.

The dark-haired fellow untied me from the wagon and led me to the farm owner. The Reds climbed into their wagon but did not leave.

"What's your name, boy?" asked the dark-haired one, who I assumed to be the overseer or farm manager or foreman.

I answered respectfully, "Matthew Little, sir. I got lost —"

"All I asked was your name, boy," he interrupted sharply. "You speak when I tell you and we'll get along fine. Who is your master?"

"I don't have a master. I'm a free man from Philadelphia. I just got lost in the woods."

"We ain't that close to Philadelphia that you coulda just got lost. What you doing here, free boy?" he demanded.

"As I was saying, I was just out walking for the day and got turned around. The more I walked, the more lost I got until the gentlemen on the wagon and their pets located me. I'd greatly appreciate it if you could direct me back to Pennsylvania."

"First thing, boy, is you ain't going back to no Pennsylvania, if that's where you from. If you don't cause no problems, you won't go nowhere. If you do cause trouble, we can get you a nice place in Miss'ssippi, maybe."

Right about there, I unwittingly made my first mistake – I tried to appeal to an overseer's sense of right and wrong.

"Isn't it against the law to enslave a free person? A simple call, I mean, letter to my employer would verify my story."

"Second thing, boy. You ain't free now, if you ever was. Best thing for you is you forget you ever heard the word free. All we know, you might be down here to steal slaves."

The overseer looked at the taller man, who raised his eyebrows and nodded slightly at the notion.

Not realizing which way the wind was blowing, I made my second mistake – I challenged an overseer's opinion.

"I don't even know where I am, so I certainly couldn't lead anyone away from here. Isn't there some way to straighten out this mix-up?"

"Third thing, boy. You need to learn to talk right. You don't sound like a nigger, and that don't make me too comfortable."

I guess I had grown overly tired of hearing criticisms of my speech, so, rather than give the intelligent reply of "Yassuh," as Harriet would have done, I regrettably slipped into 1990's mode and made my third, and ultimately most grievous mistake.

"Are Blacks limited to a specific speech pattern?" I asked rhetorically. "Is there a nigger-speak class which I missed? Can we neither vote, move about freely, nor talk in standard English? Perhaps I don't talk like a nigger because niggers only exist in the heads of the small-minded? I am an Afric. . ., a Negro and Negroes speak in as many different ways as any other inhabitants of this planet!"

When I concluded my diatribe, the semi-distinguished gentleman cleared his throat to get our attention and spoke.

"Your name again, boy?"

"Matthew Little, sir."

"Well, Matthew, I would like to welcome you to the Bates Plantation. While I would like to believe your tale about being lost, I truly cannot imagine anyone, even a nigra, being that stupid. The only conclusion I can draw is that you fancy yourself to be a Moses come to let your people go.

"I had two choices when Mr. Smith brought you to my attention. I could turn you over to the authorities, who would promptly stretch your young neck, or I could take you under my protection and allow you to live and work here. Do not make me regret being a humanitarian, boy."

I could only stand there, still literally bound hand and foot. It was obvious that no amount of talking could remedy my situation.

"Mr. Jones. Give the boy a proper welcome of ten strokes to make sure he remembers our talk."

"Yes sir, Mr. Bates," Jones said, as if his boss had asked him to go to the Polaroid machine and make ten copies of a contract. This whole indoctrination or initiation to slavery thing was just business – a business which could cost me skin unless I thought fast.

"I won't be any trouble at all, Master Bates, sir, and I appreciate your gesture on my behalf, sir. The strokes won't be necessary," I said as obsequiously as I could.

"Make that fifteen strokes, Jones," Bates said calmly. "He still hasn't learned how and when to speak to us."

Obviously, I needed to work on my servility. My choices were disgustingly limited. Shut up and let him hit me, speak up and get hit even more, or try to escape while tied up and get hit still more when caught.

Jones walked me to the barn, removed my shirt, and tied me spread-eagled to rusting metal loops on the barn. I did not struggle or resist in any way. The whole thing was utterly surreal to me, and in anticipation of what would occur, I began to silently cry.

The idea of getting whipped reminded me of the scene in the first Arnold Schwarzenegger/Woody Allen buddy flick when Arnold told Woody that he should use getting shot as motivation to get revenge, and not to just sit down and cry.

Nothing happened for a couple of minutes. I heard footsteps walking away and then returning. Then Jones walked up behind me and whispered nastily in my ear, "Remember this, boy."

I said nothing as I listened to him pace a few steps back and then stop. I flinched when he cracked the whip once, as if to warm it up. I tensed as it whistled through the air toward me, its song growing louder until it abruptly ended with a splat on my back.

"Aaaa!" I screamed as I felt skin being ripped from my back and blood began to trickle along my spine.

"Whack!" sang the whip again as it returned to my defenseless shoulders and back.

"Aaaa!" I replied softly as the note caught in my throat and took my wind.

At the third whack, just before I lost consciousness, I knew that, as Jones had commanded, I would definitely remember this.

10

Of Human Bondage

I don't generally sleep on my stomach, so I absently tried to turn onto my side. A hand on my butt and another on the back of my head pushed my face into the prickliest mattress I have ever had the displeasure of kissing. Regrettably, this also caused me to fully regain consciousness, which in turn resulted in an awareness of a pain that no being should ever have to experience.

My back and shoulders felt so raw and exposed that a simple puff of wind stung like alcohol on a deep cut. Though I tried, I could not stop myself from imagining what actual alcohol would feel like. Just the thought caused me to wince yet again in renewed pain, so I thought instead of a less irritating topical antiseptic, Mercurochrome.

That thought led to thoughts of infection control, which forced me to open my eyes and face the person who kept me from rolling over. She was a Black female, about sixteen or seventeen, of average height and build. Her hair stuck out in wisps from beneath a drab red scarf. She looked at me with soft brown eyes that were somewhat red, either from crying, lack of sleep, or both. Her mouth was tight as if she were struggling to prevent captive words from escaping.

"Thank you for keeping me from turning over. I could have really hurt myself," I said as a means of breaking the ice.

"My name is Paula," she began, "and I can tell you ain't never been whipped before, for sho. Yo back is all tore up, so massuh say you don't got to work tomorrow. Is you really a freeman? What's yo name? Does all free niggers talk like you?"

I flashed a pained smile at her. Apparently she could no longer control the floodgates as her questions spilled out. I can vaguely remember when I was her age wearing my feelings on my sleeves. Everything was still new and therefore still fascinating.

She looked at me with anticipation, expecting an intriguing answer or heart-stopping tale. Perhaps talking would help me forget the pain.

I spoke slowly at first.

"My name is Matthew Little, and yes, I was born free. Bates, however, seems of the opinion that freedom is a factor of one's geographic location rather than a birthright. And no, not every free Negro speaks like me. Of course, not every White person speaks like me either. The way a person speaks has more to do with education than skin color."

"You sho talk pretty. All I think I got from it is yo name, Matthew, and you is free. And that not every nigger talk like you."

Talking did not help with the throbbing and stinging in my back.

"Is there something you can do about this pain?" I asked.

Paula reached down and her fingers came up coated with a nasty looking, greasy concoction which she proceeded to smear lightly on my sliced up back. To my surprise, despite the noxious smell, it was instantly soothing. Knowing my treatment choices were limited, I decided not to question the salve, choosing instead blissful ignorance.

"You lucky Massuh Jones only give you five licks. Massuh Bates make him stop 'cause you pass out."

She hesitated before continuing.

"Can you read and write?"

"Yes, I can. In another life, I was a teacher. But now, I would be happy just to get back to Philadelphia and perform warehouse inventory, or even unload ships."

"Is that place with the ships up north?"

"Yes, actually not too very far from here. Do many slaves escape from here?"

"Don't talk about escaping!" Paula hissed, instantly serious. "Never. Massuh Bates say if anybody try, he kill every nigger on the place."

After my beating and the cavalier way he ordered it, I felt Bates capable of almost anything. Either he truly felt Blacks to be property or his economic investment in the plantation caused him to affect the façade in order to maintain control.

"How could he run the plantation if he killed everyone? Slaves are too expensive for him to just kill us."

"My daddy say he might just kill one person and sell the rest down south. It ain't worth some getting free when the others got to pay for it."

"How many Negroes are here?"

"Must be sixteen now with you. You ain't gonna try to escape, is you?"

"No, I suppose I can't. Not unless I take everyone with me."

She had made a good point and complicated my life by a factor of sixteen.

∂ ∂ ∂

Paula informed me that the Bates Plantation grew tobacco and not cotton, which I'd always assumed to be the crop of choice on plantations. Although she worked in the house, her father worked in the fields, which is

94

where I would also work. The workday extended from sunrise to sunset, Monday through Saturday. I hoped my first day would not be the summer solstice.

She also told me that, for the time being, I would share the cabin we were in with her, her father, and her younger brother. Her father was Mr. Thomas, the strongest man on the plantation, she said proudly. Her brother, named Nigger Boy by her father to save the White man the trouble, stayed with Grandma Sukey during the workday. Sukey's role on the plantation was to take care of the children until they were old enough to work in the house or field. Nigger Boy spent the days playing and running small errands, enjoying his last few months of relative freedom before his sixth birthday made him a commodity.

I looked around the small, fusty one-room shack and wondered what Martha Stewart and Tim the Tool Man could do with this place. The predominant color scheme was dirt on dirt, with dirt accents. My odds of acquiring some manner of infection seemed quite high.

A small rock fireplace and kitchenware took up most of one wall. Four small crates were positioned at each side of a larger crate to form a dinette of sorts. Three sleeping pallets were laid out along the wall opposite the door, with a large trunk at the head of the center bedding. My pallet made four in the small, and now, quite crowded cabin. A single window opening was opposite the fireplace. No glass filled the window slot, but a large board about the size of the opening rested on the wall below the window, apparently to be used to cover the hole during inclement weather.

At first glance the floor appeared to be just dirt, but it was actually unfinished wooden planks, many of which seemed to be nailed to the frame of the house and all of which were covered with dirt and dust. My first impulse upon looking at the floor was to sweep, sweep, sweep like the wind and, if only in that way, give the place a woman's touch, so to speak. I later decided that the dirt actually served the purpose of protecting our feet from the splintery boards. Equally significant, I also later figured out that after a hard day's work, sweeping was a low priority.

The corner behind the door had a threadbare curtain hanging limply from the ceiling. The drape formed a makeshift dressing and cleansing area, mainly used by Paula and me. Mr. Thomas and Nigger Boy were neither particularly modest nor hygienic.

Other than the contents of the trunk, the Thomases' lives and possessions were an open book. I wondered where Mrs. Thomas might be, but decided not to ask immediately, knowing from history (and Stowe's *Uncle Tom's Cabin*) how slave families were often separated.

♂ ♂ ♂

"Ain't no troublesome Negroes on the place but me, and now I reckon you," Mr. Thomas said to me in his resonant voice when he walked in and saw I was conscious. "I guess ole Massuh Bates don't want the good Negroes to get tainted by us. Yo name, suh?"

"My name is Matthew Little, sir, from Philadelphia."

"I cain't say I'm glad to have you here Matthew. I likes my privacy, but long as you stay out my business, we ain't got no problems."

"Yes sir," I said, looking up from my pallet at the tall, dark, powerfully built man.

I've known some White women who have a thing for Blacks, but I've never really fantasized about Black men. Or Black women for that matter. It's not a racial thing, but simply the fact that I've always found White skin to be more appealing. I don't even care much for the deeply suntanned look.

Perhaps because I was getting used to being around Blacks more and I was getting used to my own Black skin, I did find Mr. Thomas to be handsome. His bearing more than anything physical stood out, for I still prefer a Colin Firth or Garth Brooks to a Billy Dee Williams or Wesley Snipes. He most reminded me of Jim Brown.

Mr. Thomas did not carry himself like a slave, or how I imagined a slave would comport himself. He walked with an unexpected confidence, always looking forward or about, but never downward as I had observed of both many free Blacks and most other slaves. When he made contact with Whites, he looked them in the eye while saying yes sir and no sir, not quite challenging, but definitely indicating he felt the relationship was temporary like that of employer/employee instead of master/slave.

Mr. Thomas' grammar and vocabulary were poor, as would be expected, but there was no laziness to his speech. His voice had a way of physically touching the listener like the light vibration that a whisper directly in your ear can cause. It was like a smooth vocal blend of Charlton Heston and James Earl Jones – authoritative and deep.

Naturally, I didn't pick all of this up in the initial meeting that evening, but over time.

The days were a blur of tedious, exhausting physical labor in the fields. I felt like a human tractor bit, turning over acres of soil an inch at a time and pulling weeds. Other days were spent topping the tobacco by snapping off the nutrient-draining flower buds from both the top and bottom of the plants. Eventually, we picked the leaves of the plants, a few at a time over the course of several weeks.

Singing work songs helped make the time go by a little more pleasantly and paced us so we worked steadily but not too fast. I suspect that the U.S. labor crisis could be solved if we had work songs in our factories, and possibly even in our office buildings where data entry type tasks are performed. I'll bet the Japanese have great work songs and that's why they're kicking our butts. Or maybe not.

I introduced "Kumbayah" to the Bates Plantation, and many of us made up additional verses to make it last longer. Whoever had a new line would sing it out loudly and the others would join in after the first line. My favorites were "Drop that sun, my lord," "Let me sit, my lord," and "Gimme some grits, my lord." I also tried to introduce John Lennon's "Imagine," but the rhythm wasn't right.

Randy Newman's "Sail Away" probably would have been too dead on and gotten me whipped. But, while laboring away, I couldn't help but hear his gravelly voice sarcastically sing, "It's great to be an American."

Plantation life helped me fully understand what Maya Angelou meant when she wrote about the caged bird with the clipped wings singing of freedom. Many of our songs alluded to freedom, either earthly or in an afterlife. I remember reading in one of my friend George's books (by John Webster, I think) the similar sentiment of, "We think caged birds sing, when indeed they cry." Though we tried to have fun with our songs, our workplace was not a fun place in any way.

Most of the other slaves considered me a typical free Black, despite my attempts to explain the actual variety of Blacks in the north. My first conversations with most were punctuated with lots of "huhs" and "whats." They couldn't comprehend my vocabulary, and I couldn't always understand their accents and enunciation.

Only the driver, Ole Sam, and his son, Joseph, treated me less than civilly.

The driver on a plantation is basically a Black assistant overseer. Ole Sam took his job seriously except when it came to overseeing his own son. Every prison has its snitches I suppose, and those two were just not stand-up guys. If a field hand slowed below the standard pace, Ole Sam shouted out loudly enough for the overseer, Jones, to hear, "Git after it now nigger!" Most of us droned the standard reply of, "Yassuh Marse Sam."

I suspect Ole Sam resented the fact that my arrival had drawn attention from him, while Joseph saw me as a direct threat to his future courtship of Paula. Both Sam and Joseph took the other slaves' tolerance and fear of them for respect and love. So delusional or simple were they that when someone added the lines "Take Ole Sam" and "Joseph too" to "Kumbayah," they considered it a sign of affection.

Ole Sam always wore a brown bowler style hat and a maroon paisley vest, no matter the weather. Both items were well worn (as opposed to worn well), but they made Sam stand out among the slaves. Despite making the same sartorial statement as a lime green leisure suit and sombrero in an assembly line, Ole Sam clearly fancied he cut a dashing figure.

Although ostensibly married, Ole Sam had an eye for the ladies, including the cook, Brenda, who sort of had a thing with Mr. Thomas. I say sort of because Mr.

Thomas accepted Brenda's gifts of leftovers and sex, but without the romantic enthusiasm she plainly desired. Brenda knew that Mr. Thomas was only with her because they were the only two single slaves in their age group, but nonetheless maintained hope it would develop into something more.

One evening, after I had been a slave for about a week, Mr. Thomas asked me to go for a walk with him. We strolled down the road between the slave quarters toward the tobacco fields, not saying much until we were out of earshot of the cabins.

Then, he looked at me seriously and asked, "Do you know how to read, Matthew? And write?"

"Yes sir, I can do both quite well. Would you like to learn?"

"I don't figure I'm gone need no readin' and writin', but I figure Nigger Boy and Paula might can use it someday. Negroes ain't gone be slaves forever."

"No sir."

I couldn't tell him that slavery wouldn't be fully over until 1900 when the final stage of the Negro Emancipation Act was complete. In my studies of history in school, I saw the act as a logical way of manumission, but after just a week of these conditions, I had second thoughts. Only murderers, rapists, and child abusers deserve to live like this.

"I'd be glad to show them what I can," I said. Then, figuring this might be a good time to ask a few questions,

I asked, "So, why does everyone, even the overseer, call you Mr. Thomas?"

He chuckled. The only time I ever heard him chuckle.

"Well, boy, it all started when my last massuh first bought me. He paid a hell of a lot of money for me and my family, but we wasn't too happy about it cause our folks was still back on the ole plantation. First thing, his overseer got in my face calling me nigger and boy, shaking his whip all over the place. They must teach'em in overseer school to beat down the biggest nigger to show the other niggers it ain't no good to fight. Or maybe it just make'em feel mo' white to order a big buck around.

"Well, I was younger and mo' stubborn then and just wasn't in the mood for that, so I told him, 'My name is Mr. Thomas, suh. Please call me by my name and we won't have no trouble. I'll work hard as you need me to.'

"Well, he didn't like that too much, so he cocked back his arm and swung his little white hand at me like he was gone slap me. Like I said, I just wasn't in no mood to be a nigger that day, so I caught his hand in my hand.

"He start yelling at me, 'Nigger you better . . .,' but then he got quiet real quick cause soon as I heard that word nigger, I got mad and started squeezing his hand. I was gone kill him but I knowed that wouldn't do

102

nobody no good, but I had to do something, so I just kept squeezing.

"That cracker look in my eyes, and I guess he knowed what would happen if I stopped squeezing while I was still mad as I was, so he just dropped that whip, fell to his knees, and started crying while I broke near 'bout every bone in his hand.

"Massuh Shelby first ain't know what to do to help his overseer without killing the man he jus' paid so much money for. But then he said to me, he said, 'Mr. Thomas, I know you done had yoself a hard day today, so why don't you take yo family to that cabin over there and get settled in for work tomorrow. How 'bout that, Mr. Thomas?'

"By this time I wasn't so mad no mo', and both our hands was real sweaty and I couldn't hardly hold it no mo' anyway, so I just said, 'Yassuh massuh,' and walk off with my family.

"I could hear Massuh Shelby yelling at that ole overseer about how to deal with niggers just been took from they families, and how to look in our eyes to see what kinda nigger we is. He say the White man got to use his brain to know how to deal with niggers. He say they got to know our weaknesses to control us.

"That overseer was still crying, but he was listening. After the harvest that year, he caught my oldest boy out after the curfew and got him sold down South. I couldn't do nothing. He was gone when I woke up the next day."

He paused and looked away for nearly a minute before continuing.

"Maybe, instead of making him call me Mr. Thomas, I shoulda made him promise not to break up my family. And maybe make him pay me money for my work."

Then he got very quiet. There was nothing I could say. I wanted to hug him and say things would be okay, but they wouldn't be for a very long time.

11

Territorial Marking

E ver dream yourself into a dead end, where things just happen over and over, in a loop? That's how the plantation felt. I kept thinking, *Time to wake up*. But I could never wake up.

Things settled into an exhausting routine. Insofar as overall physical fitness goes, the manual labor aspect of slavery served as an excellent way to get in shape. My (Matthew's) body grew rock hard with decent aerobic conditioning as well. I could imagine a really bad, really tasteless comedy skit lampooning a workout guru like Richard Simmons or Jane Fonda advertising, "Whip yourself into shape with my Extreme Gardening Workout!"

The only problem with a twelve to fourteen hour workout is that it leaves little time for anything else. At least the commute was short, and I never had to worry about what to wear. Lemonade out of lemons.

Per Mr. Thomas' request, I began instructing his children each evening after work. Paula sat uncomfortably close to me during our lessons, focusing more on my face and torso than the letters and numbers I scratched in the dirt and dust. She'd repeat my words, but minutes later had no idea what we'd discussed.

On the other hand, Nigger Boy (I wished Mr. Thomas would change that name!) was a veritable sponge. He immediately caught on to the concept of different sounds for different letters combining to form words. As he learned new words, his speech pattern changed markedly. When writing a word he didn't know, he didn't hesitate to use invented spelling. Moreover, once I told him the correct spelling, he committed it to memory, almost never making the same mistake twice.

As Victor Hugo said, "To learn to read is to light a fire; every syllable that is spelled out is a spark." Someday, Boy would doubtless spark a wildfire.

While weeding in the fields and planning the night's lesson in my head, the fact that this boy would never get the opportunity to test his limits and contribute to society struck me, initially saddening, and then angering me.

The truth of the United Negro College Fund's slogan, "A mind is a terrible thing to waste," became real to me.

♂ ♂ ♂

During my third or fourth month on the plantation, Jones the overseer took a sick day. Ole Sam could barely contain his joy. He got to ride the overseer's horse and carry the whip. Everyone, including Ole Sam, knew he wouldn't use the lash unless ordered by Bates or the overseer, but it nonetheless served as some sort of twisted phallic symbol for him, making him downright giddy.

The other slaves had no particular love or respect for Ole Sam, but neither did we actively hate him. He was one of us, and if we didn't obey him in the fields, he was punished as well as whoever disobeyed him. Sam knew we could cause as much trouble for him as he could cause for us, so we all played the game.

In Jones' absence, Mr. Thomas decided to work near me, and uncharacteristically, talked while he worked. He made small talk for a bit, asking about my family, but it was obvious he was easing the conversation toward my personal life.

"I reckon you got a girl back home?" he asked as casually as he could.

"Not any more," I replied. "I was real sick for a while and nearly died. After I got better, things just weren't the same."

"Yeah. After my wife died, I didn't want to be around any other women for a long while. But I guess you can tell Paula kinda like you."

"Yes sir, but I wouldn't take advantage of your hospitality by, you know, taking advantage of your daughter. I mean, she's so young and all."

"You all must do things different up north. Paula sixteen now and it's 'bout time she found a good man. Problem is, Ole Sam's boy, Joseph, think he that man."

"I noticed that. He's mad at me just for living in the same house."

"Well, if you like Paula, and you know she like you, then, well . . ., what I'm trying to say is, Joseph ain't got no claim on her, just so you know."

"I understand what you're saying sir, and I'm flattered you think highly enough of me to . . . you know, to say you don't mind if she and I . . . become involved."

"Just be good to her and don't hurt her, boy. She still got some girl left in her, but she gone be a good woman. Anyway, I guess I better get back after it 'fore Ole Sam get ideas with that whip," Mr. Thomas said, giving me a quick wink before refocusing on his work.

Although we had never stopped weeding, once Mr. Thomas shifted away from me, he rapidly pulled ahead of me on his row. This was in part because of his superior gardening prowess, but also because I slowed nearly to a crawl, mulling what had just been said.

As I've said before, this penis thing confused the hell out of me. It was kind of like my service revolver when I worked as a cop. I carried it around with me all the time, keeping it clean and taking it out regularly to practice shooting it, but I never once used it for its intended purpose. Not that I wanted to kill anyone, but I always remained curious about how I would respond in a deadly force situation and what using deadly force would feel like.

As I wondered what it would feel like, I became aroused and realized that in a pinch, in an actual emergency, I could use my new equipment. But only if I had to. My true dilemma, other than escaping without getting anyone else injured or killed, was how to gracefully withdraw from this semi-arranged relationship without hurting anyone, and without getting hurt myself.

☙ ☙ ☙

That evening, after an exceptional supper of baked chicken and rice salvaged from the Bates table by Paula and Brenda, Mr. Thomas and Brenda left for a walk. Paula glanced at me with a shy but knowing half-smile as they left.

While she started cleaning up, I called Nigger Boy over for his nightly lesson. Several weeks before, Paula had managed to acquire three sheets of paper and a discarded pencil stub from the main house. We'd nearly used up every millimeter of space on the paper, as well as reducing the pencil to a size that would soon require tweezers to use. Before long, we would have to go back to writing in the dust and dirt on the floor.

After thirty minutes or so with Nigger Boy, it was time to work with Paula. Initially I worked with them together, but Paula was slowing the boy's progress, both due to her relative disinterest in reading and writing, and the fact that she was irregularly required to work late at the main house, causing her to miss lessons.

Apparently, Mr. Thomas discussed our conversation with Paula because she immediately suggested we take a walk and perhaps have our lesson outdoors. Knowing that she and I had to talk at some point, I agreed, though I had no idea how to approach the matter.

We drifted silently toward the tobacco fields, I suppose both thinking about what might happen next. In the past, Paula had been tastefully flirtatious, letting me know of her interest without throwing herself at me. Now that things were somewhat more serious, she was more reserved, almost to the point of shyness. Part of me found that shyness appealing, although I knew nothing could happen between us. Nonetheless, as we continued alone toward the field, my arousal became tangible.

A few yards into the field, I suggested we sit. The ground was soft, because we overturned it regularly during the day, but dry. We sat side by side and turned to look at each other simultaneously. As our eyes connected under the moonlight on that warm but breezy night, I began to suspect that something could easily happen between us if I let it. But I would not, could not let it.

"I guess your father told you about our talk today," I began, unsure where I would end.

"Um hmm," Paula said, nodding.

"Well, there may have been a misunderstanding, I mean, because I'm not sure about things since, you know, I've been free and plan to be free again as soon as I can figure out how to safely do it."

A strategy had come to me while babbling that would save face for both of us – I couldn't commit because I couldn't stay. Family and all that.

"I know you not like most boys," Paula said, shocking me because I feared for an instant she knew about my being, or at least having been a woman. "You more like a man, all grown up and serious. Not like other fellers yo age. And I know I'm not as smart with reading like girls up north probably is, but I can, I can cook and clean and take real good care of you."

"You're just fine, Paula. You're better than fine. You're pretty, and sweet, and you take real good care of me and Mr. Thomas and Boy. But I can't lead you on and then just disappear when my chance at freedom comes. I don't want to put you through that kind of hurt. I see it in your father's eyes, and it makes me sad. I can't do that to you."

"Do you know what happened to my mama? Has Daddy told you?"

"No, and I didn't want to ask. I know it's personal and it would just bring back bad memories."

"Yeah, it's hard on him. Even though he spend time with Brenda, he don't feel the same about her, and he might not ever."

She paused, trying to decide whether to tell me more. This was the most contemplative I'd ever seen Paula, and at that moment I saw in her much of what I liked about Mr. Thomas.

"The day after Nigger Boy was born," she continued, "the overseer on the last plantation made Mama go back in the field. But Boy was born real late at night and Mama ain't had no time to rest or stop her bleeding and all.

"Daddy asked him real 'spectfully if she could rest just one day. Daddy said he would work twice as hard and do enough for both of 'em. But ole Davis, that was the overseer, ole Davis never liked Daddy or any of us much after Daddy near 'bout pinched off his hand, so he said Daddy had better work twice as hard anyway, but Mama had to work too.

"That was the only time I ever seen Daddy humble hisself to a White man, asking for a day off for Mama. For all the work got done that day, he woulda been better off listening to Daddy.

"'Bout a hour or so later, 'fo the sun was even good up, everybody come back from the field. Everybody but Mama. All the men was all around Daddy. Ole Davis was draped over his horse like a dead man, bleeding like one too. I pushed my way through the men to get to Daddy. His fists and shirt was all bloody and dirty. And his mouth. Blood was dripping from his mouth like a wild animal.

"'Yo mama dead,' he told me. Tears was coming out his eyes like there wasn't no end to 'em. He looked so tired, like he couldn't lift his arms, but then he opened his arms for me to come to him. He hugged me and I hugged him for what seem like all morning. I got blood all over me but I didn't care. The men around us just stood there, some of them crying too.

"Massuh Shelby took ole Davis into the big house, and then came out and told us he was alive, but that Daddy would have to be whipped. He had the whip in his hand, but his hand was shaking. Massuh yelled at the men to tie Daddy to the whipping post by the barn, but they just stood there. He started naming men, telling 'em to do what he said or they would get whipped too, but they still just stood there. Massuh's face was so red I thought blood was just gonna come shooting out *his* skin. He looked at the men and they looked back at him, looking him in his eyes instead of at the ground like good niggas.

"Finally Massuh knew they wasn't gonna do what he said, so he told everybody take the rest of the day off and get ready for Mama's funeral. Then he told Daddy he was sorry and walked away. I think Massuh knew White folks be talking about Daddy the same way they talk about Nat Turner if he kept on. It was 'bout the only time I ever seen niggas stand up to a White man. As sad as I was about Mama, I was proud at the same time. Proud to be a nigga, I mean, a Negro, like you always tell me to say."

Tears trickled from Paula's eyes down either side of her nose into her mouth. The moonlight revealed the moisture on her face, making her whole face glisten. Unable to think of anything to say, I took her left hand in both of mine. Having lost both of my parents and my brother, I certainly had some idea of what she was experiencing.

I had no handkerchief, so I removed my right hand from hers and used it to try to wipe the tears from her eyes. She smiled softly at me, a sad smile that said thanks for caring enough to try to comfort me and make me feel better about something for which there can be no comforting, and about which I can never feel better.

Our eyes connected and it was clear that Paula needed a hug. I needed one too, so I gently pulled her to me. Because we were still sitting, our bodies were at an awkward angle to each other, so we both rolled onto our knees and faced each other to allow for a more full embrace.

If men are from Mars and women are from Venus, I wonder from what place are we who are not exactly men or women. I still thought of myself as a woman. After 41 years of womanhood and less than a year in a man's body, that was only natural. However, I was beginning to understand a bit about why men are so fucked up.

A full ninety percent or more of me felt nothing but maternal feelings toward Paula, wanting only to give her a shoulder on which to lean, a friendly hand to hold. That other ten percent, though, reacted to the touch of her silken cheek against my face, her firm breasts pressing on my chest, and her pelvis brushing mine. I knew that I should do something to avoid a misunderstanding, so, against the urgings of my egocentric penis, I eased my pelvis away from Paula's.

Too late were my actions. Paula removed her head from my shoulder and tilted it back, eyes closed and lips puckered. My penis eloquently argued that it would be positively rude to leave her in that position, so I kissed her, at first chastely but gradually less chastely and more urgently.

My other head, functioning poorly now with a sub-optimal blood supply, gradually realized that this was probably wrong, so it took control of the situation after an intense minute or so. Breathing heavily and taking a step back on my knees, I asked, "So, uh, who was this

Nat Turner that you said your father might be compared to if Master Shelby tried to whip him?"

"For sho you not like most boys, Matthew," gasped Paula, grinning sweetly at me while looking up and down my body, with her eyes settling just below my waist. "But you not as different as you try to act, either."

I could not offer a credible denial to her observation, so I mutely waited for her to answer my question. Turner had only rated a sentence or two in the fifth-grade history books, and therefore I knew almost nothing about him.

"So, maybe ten years 'fo I was born, a Negro in Virginia, Nat Turner, got a bunch of slaves to follow him and they killed more than fifty White people 'fo they was caught and killed. I'm amazed word about Nat ain't reach up north. What he did made some White folks scared to push us too far, and made other White folks want to kill us any time we do anything wrong, figuring we gone be the next Nat. Funny thing is, it made some niggas, Negroes, more bold and some more afraid. I cain't decide if it was a good thing or a bad thing, but it made everybody think."

"Thinking is almost always good," I said, looking at her looking at me. "I guess we'd better head back inside or I'm going to have to tell Ole Jones I'm too sleepy to work tomorrow."

Paula giggled at the idea. Personal days aren't typically part of the slavery benefits package.

116

We headed back to the cabin huddled together for warmth, among other things. I was uncertain whether I'd resolved anything, and moreover, felt conflicted about whether I wanted to.

One of the benefits of having been a police officer is a heightened awareness of my surroundings. Though I saw no one, I knew we were being watched on the walk back, but the watcher was being careful not to be seen by us, so I assumed he or she was choosing to respect our privacy. As it happens, the watcher was just being sneaky.

♂ ♂ ♂

The next day, as we lined up for our bread, fatback, and water, Joseph, the pompous son of the driver, Ole Sam, asked if I would join him under a tree a few yards away from the main cluster of workers. Curious, and with no other pressing scheduling conflicts, I accepted.

Joseph didn't beat around the bush. After we sat down, he immediately took a large bite of bread and meat for confidence and asked, while chewing, "So you courting Paula now?"

The watcher hadn't waited long to reveal himself.

If I had it to do again, I would have said no and been done with it. Something about the way he spoke though, accusingly, with food particles flying, as if Paula and I had transgressed by failing to obtain his permission to speak, something about his incongruously haughty manner triggered my smart aleck switch. This switch is

117

probably one of the less desirable side effects of seven years of police work.

Joseph continued to wolf down his food and drink, while glaring at me with his round young face in a manner which I suppose was intended to intimidate.

Instead, it mostly amused.

I smiled softly and looked him directly in the eyes to let him know that his attempt at intimidation was failing miserably. Then I took a bite of bread and meat, sipped a bit of water, and said, "Well, I wouldn't go so far as to say we are courting, but it's only natural that two people who live in the same cabin and spend a good deal of time together would become close. She is an attractive woman, which I suppose you've noticed also."

My words were intended to imply more was going on than was really going on. They seemed to succeed, as Joseph grew more agitated, breathing harder and masticating with renewed aggression.

Pleased with my verbal victory, I rose and turned away from him to leave.

Displeased with me in general, Joseph decided to escalate matters, weakly shoving me from behind. As I stumbled forward, I kicked backwards awkwardly, striking his upper thigh. Then I spun and landed a roundhouse hammer fist to his temple and an elbow solidly into his solar plexus.

As he fell to his knees, I walked away to finish my lunch.

I heard him call after me softly, "You just got here. I been with her since we was kids. You cain't have her. She was born to be with me."

12

Bad Things Sometimes Happen to Good People

In hindsight, I don't know whether my bigger mistake was teaching Nigger Boy how to read or punching out Joseph.

Okay, so the punching wasn't such a bright idea.

I'm not sure why I was so aggressive. I hadn't struck anyone in well over a decade. Since the eighties. But I guess it's like riding a bike, even with a different body. I'd never completely lost the reflexes I'd developed as an officer.

Or possibly testosterone overrode my brain or at least nudged me in that direction. Matthew's body, my body that is, was bound to have heaps of testosterone coursing through it at that age.

Anyway, Mr. Thomas and I had warned Paula and Nigger Boy to neither discuss reading nor to read in the presence of anyone else, but somehow word of the lessons got to Joseph. After our dust-up, Joseph wanted more than ever to get rid of me, so he told the overseer Jones, and naturally, Jones told Master Bates.

What I wouldn't give for a good dictionary to find out the etymology of the word masturbate. Is it a word that hadn't come into common use at this time or were these guys pretending that it didn't exist? I just don't think I would own a plantation (or a motel either for that matter) if my name were Bates.

Anyway, Paula came running home out of breath one Sunday afternoon, tears covering her face.

"Massuh gone sell you and Boy," she panted at me. Looking at her father, she repeated, "He gone sell Boy and Matthew, Daddy!"

"Why you think that, girl?" Mr. Thomas asked, frowning.

"Mr. Jones say Joseph tell him Nigger Boy and Matthew can read. Massuh say he gotta sell'em."

"Shit. Shit, shit, shit," was all I could think to say. A wave of panic peppered with guilt swept through me. My mind raced. Should we run, hide, eviscerate Joseph? Shit.

Ultimately, all I could do was say to Mr. Thomas, "I'm sorry."

"Where Nigger Boy?" Mr. Thomas asked softly.

"I don't know," Paula whimpered, "but we'll get him."

He was just outside Ole Sam's cabin, playing with another young boy and girl. As Paula and I approached him, we saw Jones in the distance coming from the big house toward us. I knew then that running wasn't an option.

We told Boy that Mr. Thomas wanted to see him right now and beat Jones to the cabin by a minute at most.

Mr. Thomas, as usual, was brief in talking to Nigger Boy. "Somebody told Massuh that you and Matthew can read, so Massuh gone sell y'all. I'ma try to get Massuh to change his mind, but I don't know if he will. Jones coming, so listen to what Matthew say, like he your Daddy. Be a man."

I looked Mr. Thomas in the eye, and swore, "Whatever happens, I'll take care of Boy. We'll be back. I promise."

He nodded.

Jones opened the door without knocking. He avoided Mr. Thomas' eyes, ordering Boy and me to come with him.

"I'm coming too," Mr. Thomas stated firmly.

"Master Bates only want them two —"

"I'm coming."

Jones wisely decided to shut up and led us out to the barn where Bates awaited. Mr. Thomas and Paula followed silently.

৪ ৪ ৪

"Can you read, boy?" Bates asked me.

"No suh," I replied as subserviently as I could.

"Who taught the other boy to read?"

"I don't know, suh. I'm pretty sure he can't read either."

"Come here, boy," Bates said to Nigger Boy. He showed him a piece of paper with some words on it. "What does this say?"

Nigger Boy looked at his father and then me. I shook my head slightly to let him know he shouldn't read it.

"Read it, boy!" commanded Bates.

Boy was plainly scared and looked away from the paper.

"Read it, boy, and I'll give you some chicken."

Boy glanced our way, but said nothing.

"Read the words or Jones is going to beat your father to within an inch of his life."

Boy's eyes widened, but Mr. Thomas shook his head at Boy.

"This is your last chance. Read it or I'm going to shoot your sister."

Mr. Thomas stiffened as Bates reached behind his back and pulled a handgun from the waist of his trousers. Paula froze.

I wanted to believe that Bates was bluffing, but if anything happened to Paula, I wouldn't be able to live with myself.

"He, he can't read it sir, but I might be able to make out a word or two, sir," I volunteered.

"It's too late for you, boy!" Bates snapped at me. "I'd shoot you now, but that would be money out of my pocket. The child reads it or the girl dies."

"Try to read it," Mr. Thomas told a tearful Boy.

"Yes sir," Boy mumbled.

He took the paper and haltingly recited, "Slaves, obey your earthly masters with fear and trembling, with a sincere heart, as you would Christ."

Boy sounded out words that I had never taught him, only totally mangling 'sincere' and 'Christ.' I was both proud and frightened.

Bates glared at me, and less severely at Mr. Thomas. Utilizing slave owner logic, he chided us about how niggers reading could never lead to any good.

The smart aleck in me wanted to ask, "Why is reading such a big deal? Are you afraid we'll skip over to the neighborhood Slave Branch of the library, dash to the Emancipation section, and read our way out of bondage?"

But I'd finally learned when to keep my big mouth shut.

Jones shackled Boy and me together and led us toward the main house. Mr. Thomas and Paula walked alongside in silence.

Again I told them, "We'll be back. Don't give up hope. I promise, we'll be back."

Mr. Thomas nodded, but I could tell he wasn't going to hold out hope. Paula looked me in the eyes and nodded softly, needing to believe me.

As Ole Sam maneuvered a buckboard wagon to the main house, Paula hugged both of us tightly and kissed each of us on the forehead. Mr. Thomas shook my hand wordlessly. Then he got on his knees, pulled Boy to him, and held him for about a minute. I couldn't tell if he was trying to transfer some of his strength to his son, or absorb his child's essence. No tears were shed, but the emotions radiated strongly from them. I would have cried, but I knew Mr. Thomas wouldn't have wanted it, and Boy needed me to be strong.

When Mr. Thomas released Boy, we were immediately loaded in back. Jones climbed into the front with Ole Sam.

♂ ♂ ♂

We rode south to town, where we were jailed until the following morning. No food, and no turn down service, but no mistreatment either.

"Are we really gonna see Daddy and Paula again?" Boy asked when we were alone in the cell.

"I promised your Daddy, so I guess we will. Don't want him getting mad at me for breaking a promise."

"Good."

"Did I ever tell you the story of Hansel and Gretel?"

"No."

"Well, once upon a time . . ." I began.

Boy stayed awake just long enough to hear the happily ever after and then slipped peacefully off to sleep.

Although he cried softly in his sleep, he seemed to be handling this as well as any six-year-old could.

ℰ ℰ ℰ

Morning brought a cup of water and a chunk of bread for each of us. Boy asked so many questions about the story that I ended up retelling it, extending the happy ending for his sake.

A little past midday, voices in the outer area filtered back to us, indicating our ride was here.

We were again shackled and loaded onto a wagon, this time with three other Black men and two Black women. No one said a word. The wagon driver was a boy of about ten or eleven years old.

The man who escorted us out of jail turned to face us. As he cradled a shotgun in his arms and patted the revolver at his side, he said, "Y'all is going south now. Most times, that means you did something to rile your master. Since y'all is money to me, I ain't gonna try to kill you if you cause trouble unless I have to. I'm just gone shoot off a finger or part of a foot and let you hurt the rest of the ride. If you good though, I'll feed you twice a day 'til we get to Georgia."

Then he turned around and directed the boy to begin driving. We looked to be headed generally westward, if I was reading the sun properly.

Our mobility in the wagon was limited as our shackles were looped through metal rings attached to the side and floorboards. Unlike modern day handcuffs, our shackles were made from heavy, black wrought iron with an eighteen inch or so length of chain fettering our hands and feet. The only padding we had to protect us from the jolting wagon was our own clothing. Uncomfortable would be an understatement.

When we were under way, I introduced Boy and myself to the other passengers. They nodded and mumbled their names, but not much more.

After a bit, Boy asked for a story. Knowing we were in for a long ride, I opted for a longer tale and began telling a variation on my favorite book of all time, *Watership Down*.

After an hour of narration, my mouth and throat grew dry, so I asked our transporters for a sip of water.

The boy driving the wagon had plainly been listening to the story and tossed me a canteen.

"Maybe you want to give'em some of your Momma's chicken too? And a hot bath and a shave?" the boy's father mocked sarcastically.

Turning to me, he bellowed, "Take your mouth offa my son's canteen! They's a barrel of water for you niggers under that blanket, boy."

"Yes sir," I said, handing the container back to the boy with a nod to thank him for trying.

After wetting my throat via the less than stellar beverage service, I continued my rendition of Richard Adams' story. Everyone, including the boy's father, was listening but pretending not to. Boy interrupted a couple of times to ask what a word meant or why a rabbit would or wouldn't take a certain action, but no one else said a word to me or each other until the story's end.

Shortly after sunset, we stopped for the evening. Boy was unshackled just long enough to help gather firewood. The rest of us remained chained in the wagon.

After our transporters had eaten, and the father partook of a postprandial cocktail or three, the boy served us hardtack and jerky.

"Excuse me sir, but may I be unshackled long enough to uh, you know, urinate?" I asked.

"What?" the father asked.

"Take a leak, a whiz, drain the bladder, visit the outhouse, as it were?"

"Yeah, uh, yeah," he said with a slight slur. "One at a time. But if any one of you tries to run, I'll shoot you in the legs and let you bleed to death where you fall."

Then, focusing on me, he threatened, "And storyteller. If you try anything, the boy suffers."

"Understood, sir," I said, knowing this might be my best chance to fulfill my promise to Mr. Thomas, but also realizing this could be my best chance to get us both killed.

So I just relieved myself and returned to the wagon. Maybe tomorrow.

13

Between Scylla and Charybdis

O nce we were on the road again the next morning, the son turned to me and asked, "Are you going to tell your brother another story?"

"I suppose so, uh, what's your name?" I replied, not bothering to correct the assumption that Boy and I were related.

"I'm Billy Chaney, and my daddy is —"

"Mr. Chaney, or sir, to you niggers," the boy's father interrupted. "And if you gotta tell another damn story, nigger, make it with real people and not some damn rabbits running all over the damn place. Ain't never heard of no damn rabbits doing all that stuff."

"Yes sir, Mr. Chaney. And my name is Matthew, sir."

This time I opted for Jack London's *The Call of the Wild*. I knew it would be published in the very early 1900s, but I figured there was little likelihood any of the wagon's occupants would recall my tale over 40 years hence and make a connection.

The story of a dog stolen away from his owner and sold into slavery in the Yukon was clearly more to Chaney's liking.

"Ain't nothing worse than a man stealing another man's dog or horse," Chaney commented, completely missing the hypocrisy of his stated belief and his occupation.

Later, he proceeded to explain to Billy the art of judging, buying, and trading niggers. As I listened to his teachings, I could tell Chaney seemed convinced of his superiority to Blacks, and of the bestial nature of Blacks.

Billy was clearly less than convinced, which might explain why he was on this trip.

I wondered if Chaney had always embraced the bigoted viewpoint, or if he'd experienced a time of uncertainty as Billy seemed to be, and had instead grown into that way of thinking over time. Just as children initially accept their parents' traditions and beliefs without question, Chaney may have never thought to question the Black condition. At some point, the presumed inferiority of the Negro simply became a fact in the minds of many, and not just a theory or a rationalization for slavery.

⚮ ⚮ ⚮

"So why you being sold South?" began Michael, the slender but muscular young man chained beside me.

"Reading. I taught Boy here to read, so we're both being sent away. Boy's father and sister are still in Maryland. How about you?"

"Trying to escape. Massuh wouldn't let me see my girl on the next plantation no more cuz he wouldn't get to keep our baby if we had one. Caught me at the river. I cain't swim and couldn't find no place to walk across."

"We was escaping too," said a bearded man in his thirties, pointing to himself and his wife. "Dogs caught us next morning. After massuh whipped us, he put us back to work, but a few days later, we was sold."

"What about y'all?" Michael asked the last couple.

"Massuh's wife made him sell my sister here. He went home with a black eye after I caught him trying to have his way. I guess Missus made him tell the truth, and she ain't want no truth nowhere on her plantation."

"Shaddup, niggers," yelled Chaney. "I'm getting a headache listening to y'all whining."

My hunch was that the actual source of his headache was a hangover, but I knew to bite my tongue when at the disadvantage. Chaney didn't want the truth anywhere on his wagon either.

⚮ ⚮ ⚮

Shortly before sunset, Chaney stopped to set up camp in a clearing off the main road.

132

Billy gathered wood and started a nice fire while Chaney unhitched the horses and sipped an aperitif from a worn hip flask. Once the fire was blazing nicely, Chaney prepared their meal, enjoying several more drinks both during and afterwards. By the time Billy fed us, Chaney was, as my brother Eliot used to say, cutting some serious Z's.

We'd been on the road for a day and a half, moving farther and farther away from freedom. Knowing this was probably going to be my best chance at escape, I called Billy over.

"Do you go to school?"

"Not no more. Daddy says I got as much school as he got, so it's time for me to earn my keep."

"Did you want to keep going to school?"

"Kinda. I mean I like stories, hearing'em and reading'em. I think I might even like to write'em too."

"Do you believe Black people, Negroes, are just animals, like your father says?"

The youngster paused before answering, actually giving the matter serious consideration.

"Y'all the first ones I ever really talked to. But I ain't never talked with no animals, so I guess y'all ain't exactly animals."

"Do you have slaves?" Boy asked, looking directly into Billy's eyes.

"No. We ain't rich. We just move'em around for the rich folks."

"Can I go pee now?" I asked the child, trying not to feel guilty for planning to take advantage of him. I was really beginning to like this kid, but I couldn't let my fondness for him jeopardize my goal.

"I better ask Daddy. He's gonna want to watch so you don't run."

I looked at him as innocently as I could, saying, "I can't go anywhere without Boy, and I know what your Daddy would do to him if I tried. I just don't want to piss in my pants. Please?"

Billy paused to think for a few seconds and then went to get the keys from his sleeping father. Chaney was out cold and didn't even stir when Billy unhooked the keys from his father's belt.

My escape plan was only half formed. I knew I'd have to take the keys from Billy, but I didn't want to hurt him.

Billy unchained me from the restraining loops on the wagon and motioned for me to proceed to the brush. In order to overpower Chaney, even in his inebriated state, I knew I needed more freedom, so I whispered to Billy that I needed to defecate and couldn't do it with my legs in shackles.

He again considered my dilemma for a few seconds, but ultimately decided to trust me. Just as he'd unlocked my legs and I'd gotten off the wagon, we all froze upon hearing a rustling in the woods just behind Chaney. When Billy turned to look, I took the opportunity to scramble away unseen behind a tree, my wrists still in the heavy, oversized handcuffs.

Three disheveled White men emerged from the woods, one of them brandishing an old single-shot flintlock pistol.

He was the smallest of the three, but came across as being the leader. He kicked Chaney sharply in the side and ordered him to get up.

Chaney, disoriented from the combination of drowsiness and drink, was slow to respond. Misinterpreting sluggishness for resistance, the tallest man took a turn kicking Chaney.

Billy shouted for the man to stop and started running over from the wagon to assist his father. The third interloper, a hefty, bearded man, blocked Billy's path, and then grabbed his arms.

Billy screamed and kicked at his captor, who in turn slapped Billy on the side of the head. When Chaney saw that, he snapped out of his stupor, gathered himself, and took a step toward his son.

The tall guy was about to intercept Chaney when the little guy unexpectedly shot Chaney in the right thigh. Chaney screamed and fell to the ground, clutching his bleeding leg while Billy frantically struggled to free himself.

So much for escape plan number one.

"Get his money, Zeke!" yelled the shooter to the tall guy. "I'll check on the niggers and harness the horses."

I knew Zeke would also find Chaney's revolver, and at some point the shotgun would be located. My window of opportunity for taking action would slam shut once the highwaymen had more weaponry.

Holding my loose wrist chains to prevent them from jangling, I scanned the area for a large stick to use as a combat baton. I still remembered the kata from the training academy for a three-on-one confrontation, but hoped I could improve the odds by taking out the leader straightaway. I got lucky, immediately finding a nice solid branch about two feet long. All I had to do was wait for the little guy to come closer.

When he put down his empty pistol to check the prisoners' chains, I tiptoed from behind the tree and teed off hard on the back of his skull with the branch. Apparently, not hard enough.

Instead of collapsing gently to the ground as I'd hoped, he staggered sideways and groaned before falling to one knee. His groan brought all eyes on me.

The bear of a man holding Billy shoved him to the ground and trudged heavily toward me.

The tall robber, Zeke, had just found Chaney's pistol and, odds were, he would use it on me in short order.

Now free, Billy ran straight to his wounded father, blocking the now armed Zeke for an extra second. I took that time to charge and tackle the human grizzly, using him for cover. We rolled on the ground for a few seconds and then bounced to our feet to face off.

I made sure to keep him positioned between Zeke's pistol and me. He threw a heavy but clumsy fist at me, which I parried. Then I quickly grabbed his wrist, pulling it toward me with my right hand. Straightening his arm, I banged the back of his elbow as hard as I could with my left forearm, displacing the joint. He cried out in pain and fell to his knees, unfortunately giving Zeke a clean shot at me. Realizing this, I ducked down, punching the big guy in the nose with my elbow on the way down.

Two shots whizzed over our heads. The third struck flesh and bone.

"Shit, Zeke!" yelled my opponent from his knees, because the third shot had struck him in the left shoulder.

"Sorry Mac!" Zeke yelled back. "Get down so I can kill the nigger."

I grabbed Mac by the shoulders, hoping to use him as a shield until Zeke ran out of bullets.

Instead of continuing to shoot at us from a distance, Zeke left Chaney and Billy to get an unobstructed shot at me. I hesitated, uncertain whether my best bet would be to try for a quick dash to the woods, or to continue using Mac as a shield a little longer and try to disarm Zeke when he got close enough.

Just then, Billy screamed at Zeke, "Stop right there and drop that pistol!" The boy had found Chaney's shotgun beneath the blanket where Chaney had passed out earlier.

Zeke turned, saw the shotgun, and laughed nervously.

"You don't want to shoot me, boy," he said in a soothing tone. "I ain't gonna hurt you and your daddy. We just want your money and the niggers."

"Your friend already shot Daddy. Drop the gun," Billy demanded in a shaky voice. Tears were rolling down his face, but he held the heavy weapon reasonably steady as he aimed it at Zeke.

As if things weren't crazy enough, just then Boy yelled out, "Look out Matthew!"

I wheeled around and saw the little robber, who I'd hoped would remain incapacitated from my earlier blow. While still woozy, he was nevertheless aiming his pistol at me and the already wounded Mac and pretty much everything in our general vicinity.

"Kill him, Ned! That nigger broke my arm!" Mac said.

"Don't kill nobody, Ned," Zeke said calmly, now trying to negotiate on two fronts. "That nigger is worth a lot of money alive. Just keep him there."

I watched Zeke and Billy's standoff with one eye and Ned with the other eye. Zeke was easing toward Billy a few inches at a time, but there were still about 5 yards between them.

"Billy," I said. "If he takes another step toward you or points his gun at you, shoot him. He can't sell you or your daddy, but you could get him put in jail. Don't worry about me. Ned's gun is empty."

Hearing that and realizing the truth, Ned said, "Shit," and threw the weighty weapon at me.

Instinctively, I pivoted Mac between me and Ned, with Mac absorbing the full impact of the pitched pistol with his face. With blood flowing from his forehead, nose, and mouth, as well as from the shoulder wound, Mac gurgled a moan and became dead weight falling backward on top of me.

Ned charged at me in a shambling, zombie kind of way, spewing profanity and saliva. As I tried to dislodge myself from underneath the unconscious bulk of Mac, I clawed for the empty pistol, inches beyond my reach, hoping to use it as a club to finish off the lurching Ned.

Out of the blue, adding to the tumult, from my position on the ground, I both heard and felt horses approaching.

Zeke must have heard them too. He spun away from Billy toward me, attempting to line up a clear shot.

I slid free from beneath Mac toward Ned just as Zeke fired. Blood spattered in my face as the bullet struck Mac's other shoulder. I scrambled to my feet, trying to collect Ned's empty firearm, but couldn't hold on to it with Mac's blood all over my hands. Running as if my life depended on it, which it did, I tackled Ned low, and then swiftly rolled away from him toward the cover of the trees.

As I hightailed it, I heard a shotgun blast and at least five other shots ring out at almost the same instant. One of the shots struck the tree I was trying to reach to hide behind. I zigged left and zagged back to the right to reach the tree relatively unscathed.

Hearing no more gunfire, I peered around the tree.

Zeke appeared quite dead from my perspective. Ned and Mac were at the very least, down for the count. The other slaves, along with Billy and Chaney, were alive.

Four men on horseback, three White and one Black, were putting guns away and surveying the scene.

My initial impression was that they were law enforcement and I needed to relate the story to them. I stopped myself when I realized they might only be more competent bandits.

Then another thought struck me. I'm not just another witness if they are the police – I'm a Black slave witness, and by talking to them, I'm right back where I started.

Observation struck me as the best tack for the moment.

ʃ ʃ ʃ

An older White man, a little under six feet tall with narrow shoulders, thin lips and a high forehead, seemed to be in charge. He ordered two men to watch Ned and Mac, while another pried the shotgun out of Billy's hands and attended to Chaney. The old man took his handgun out as he approached Zeke.

140

Keeping his gun trained on Zeke, he picked up the pistol at Zeke's side. He must have determined that Zeke was definitely dead because he put away his own pistol and checked the bandit's pockets.

Next, he approached Ned and Mac. Somehow, after all he'd been through, Mac was still alive.

The old man pronounced, "And he that stealeth a man, and selleth him, if it be found with him, shall die the death." Then he shot Mac in the head.

Finally, he strode to Chaney and demanded, "Give me the keys."

"What keys?" asked Chaney.

"The keys to the irons," he replied, pointing to the wagon.

"Oh, them slaves is mine to take to Georgia," Chaney declared. "I got the papers on the wagon."

"They are God's children and not the property of any earthly being. Give me the keys."

"Who do you think you are, taking my goods? You cain't —"

"I am the man who saved your life," interrupted the old man. "I am the man who still holds your life in his hands. I am the man who will free these people with or without your help. Give me the keys so that we may avoid any further bloodshed or conflict."

Chaney assessed the man and his own position for a few seconds. Reluctantly, he checked his belt and patted his pockets, searching for the keys that Billy had borrowed earlier. He shrugged his shoulders to indicate he couldn't find the keys, but then Billy reached into his own pocket and shyly handed the keys over.

As the old man approached the wagon, I realized I had seen him, or someone who looked much like him, before. Not in this timeline, but in my other lifetime. I couldn't place him immediately though.

He released Boy first. Boy scrambled down and began looking around for me.

"He's over there, behind the tree," our emancipator said, pointing at my tree.

I stepped out and walked toward Boy.

"Is you okay?" he asked. "You all bloody."

"I'm fine. Just a little battered and bruised. Are you okay? Was anyone on the wagon hurt?"

"No. We all okay. We copacetic," he said, smiling because he'd used a new word I'd taught him.

Oddly enough, an old drunkard that I arrested many years ago taught me the word. He'd fallen and couldn't get up, in part due to a minor injury and in part due to overindulgence of the grape. I was the first officer on the scene, and when I asked if he was okay, he studied my face, smiled cheerfully, and pronounced in an almost Shakespearean tone, "Lovely young policewoman, I am entirely copacetic, except for my dignity."

To paraphrase Art Linkletter, drunks say the darnedest things.

142

Once everyone was unchained, the old man, sounding like a revival preacher, announced to the Blacks, "Stand fast therefore in the liberty wherewith Christ hath made us free, and be not entangled again with the yoke of bondage. You belong to no master, or mistress, but to yourselves, and you are free!"

"Now, now hold on a minute there, mister," Chaney shouted. "I told you these here niggers is mine. I got papers!"

"And I have God and the Bible on my side. And if necessary, this," our liberator said, patting his sidearm. "I ask you not to orphan your brave son, sir, but to accept your losses and be thankful to be alive."

Chaney, who was almost completely sober after the evening's drama, simmered for nearly a minute. Looking at Billy, he nodded to the old man and pulled his son close with one arm.

Addressing the slaves, the old man began quietly. "I cannot see you to the end of your journey to freedom. Follow the North Star at night and avoid the main roads during the day. If you travel in the mornings, keep the sun to your right. In the afternoon, keep the sun to your left. I can give you a few supplies and food, and my prayers."

We all shook the hands of our rescuers, thanking them profusely.

As Boy and I gathered supplies and tied them into bundles, I couldn't get over the nagging feeling that I knew the old guy. Finally, just before hitting the road, I approached him.

"Excuse me, sir, but I feel like we've met somewhere before. What's your name?"

"I doubt that we have met, but my name is Brown, son. John Brown."

Not thinking, I mumbled, "Harper's Ferry."

Brown's blue-gray eyes opened wide and his body tensed.

"What did you say, son?"

Realizing my mistake, I replied, "Nothing. Just uh . . . pondering our route."

Though I was never a history buff, I knew the basics about John Brown's attack on the Harper's Ferry armory and the guerilla attacks afterward. Brown and his followers allegedly killed over a thousand people, nearly precipitating a war within the nation over slavery.

Brown motioned over two of his men.

"This man will come with us."

"Thanks, but I've got to get Boy here back to his family and get myself back to my family in Philadelphia," I objected.

"The boy will come with us too," Brown told his men.

Boy and I were escorted away from the other slaves. It went without saying that we were once again prisoners, thanks to my big mouth.

14

Out of the Frying Pan

Brown hoisted Boy onto his horse next to the saddle horn, while I was told to ride with another of Brown's men. We met up with the rest of Brown's party on the main road at a farm wagon fitted with a canvas cover. Boy was transferred to the wagon, but I was kept on horseback.

My horse mate was a tall Black man in his forties named Dangerfield Newby. After polite introductions, we chatted amiably about family and the events of the evening, both of us pretending I wasn't a captive.

Newby told me he was from Virginia, but had been freed and now lived in Ohio. His wife and seven children, however, still lived in bondage in Virginia. His hope was that they would reunite when slavery was abolished.

His tone projected a confidence that emancipation was imminent.

I gave him the Reader's Digest condensed version of how I had traveled south from Philadelphia with Harriet Tubman, only to be captured, enslaved, and ultimately sold.

"You know Harriet Tubman?" Newby inquired in a somewhat skeptical tone.

"Yeah. We first met after a talk she gave to the Philadelphia Vigilance Committee, and a couple of days later, I followed her into Maryland."

Newby became silent, mulling my story. Then he urged our horse forward to pull alongside Brown.

"Captain Brown, sir. The boy says he knows Harriet Tubman."

"Do you truly know her?" Brown asked me, his piercing gray-blue eyes meeting mine as if to hold me to the truth.

"We aren't best friends or anything, but yes, I know her. As I told Mr. Newby, I met her in Philadelphia after a talk she gave, and a few days later, followed her to Maryland where I was captured leading slavers away from her."

"Well, I too know her. We shall talk more later."

ȣ ȣ ȣ

Newby and I rode on companionably, continuing our small talk about his family, and my experiences in Pennsylvania and on Bates' plantation.

Every time I looked at Boy, he was pointing at something or someone, and talking nonstop. It suddenly struck me that this was the closest he'd ever been to being free.

After only a few of hours of steady riding, we approached a town called Chambersburg in Pennsylvania. Newby and I and two others remained on the outskirts of town, while Brown, the wagon, and one other horseman continued into town, disappearing into the night.

When I asked what they were doing, Newby would only reply that they were getting supplies. I could only guess what supplies were being gathered under cover of night.

All returned within an hour or so. We proceeded away from town for another hour before stopping to make camp for the remainder of the night.

I wasn't tied or handcuffed, but Boy and I were kept separated. He slept on the wagon surrounded by Brown and two others, while I was placed between Newby and the other two men. They needn't have bothered worrying about me escaping on that night. I fell asleep in seconds and didn't awaken at all until Boy shook me by my sore shoulders.

"Time for breakfast, Matthew," he said happily.

Despite being somewhat disoriented, the smell of bacon and coffee snapped me to alertness, and the need to relieve myself motivated me to get moving. I felt like one giant walking bruise from the previous evening's scuffle. Although I was being held against my will, I nevertheless felt freer than I had in months.

"I'm going to go pee," I told Boy loudly enough for the others to hear. "Stay here."

He nodded, and I headed far enough into the woods to allow me to discreetly do more than just pee, selecting a nice wide tree to use as a screen for modesty's sake. For the umpteenth time, I cursed the lack of toilet paper, even the cheap, rough one-ply stuff. Green leaves were present, thankfully, but soon only autumn leaves would be available. *O Mr. Whipple, where art thou?*

After breakfast, Brown directed Boy back to the covered wagon, and placed me on horseback with his son, Owen.

Owen was a gregarious, oddly upbeat redhead with prominent, protruding ears and a sly grin not quite hidden behind his rough beard. At 35 years of age, he was third oldest of Brown's six living sons, and he had five younger sisters. Other siblings had died of various causes. Owen considered himself a farmer. Leathery skin, rough hands, and a solid build confirmed an outdoor life of hard work, but an injured right arm made him look older than his years.

148

"Do you hate White people for enslaving you?" was the first question he asked me after a lull in the conversation, which up to that point had been pretty superficial.

"Wow. I never really thought about hating a whole group of people based on their skin color. I feel a certain connectedness, almost familial, to Whites, and some of my best friends have been White."

"But do you not sometimes wish you could kill the master or the overseer?"

"Yes, in a pinch, I could see myself killing either of them. Certainly, they have wronged me, and many others, in ways that humans should not have to endure, but they are individuals. They don't represent a race of people any more than you or I. Do you hate Whites? Or Blacks?"

Owen smiled and nodded.

"You are right that you do not represent all Blacks. Your response is more thoughtful than that of most, Black or White. Regrettably, I am sometimes ashamed of being White. Nonetheless, I would not trade places with you.

"Father has made me feel at times that any White who is for slavery, or is not actively fighting against it, should be hated. In Kansas, I killed with hatred in my heart, but I am learning to look at matters more objectively. I harbor less enmity. Now there is just more confusion, more sadness and disappointment in my fellow man."

We exchanged a look of shared understanding and quietly continued on our way.

The view was incredible from horseback of the hills and mountains. All of the colors of summer were still in evidence, but the weather was that perfect blend of summer and fall.

"What is that river called?" I asked Owen as we rounded a bend and a body of water came into view. I knew we were in Maryland, but beyond that, I was lost.

"Oh, that is the old Potomac."

"It's beautiful."

"Yeah, I guess it is," Owen replied. "Seems we are so focused on what we have to do, we do not really see what's around us."

"Many people don't. Because I'm new here, I guess I still have the eyes of a child."

"Mayhap," Owen agreed.

"I read somewhere that George Washington was so strong that he was able to throw a silver dollar across the Potomac. That's a mighty big river, so I'm guessing that story is just a myth."

"Most assuredly. As is the tale of him chopping down a cherry tree at age six."

"Now I've seen the painting of him standing up in the boat as he and his troops crossed the icy Delaware, so surely that is no myth," I joked.

"I would wager old Washington didn't pose like that for some artist. And if he did, the men in the boat probably just wanted him to sit down before they all went face first into that cold water," he laughed.

Picturing a boatload of panicked soldiers, I joined him in laughter. Owen didn't seem at all like a killer, but he had already confessed to killing in Kansas, with the promise of more bloodshed after the upcoming Harper's Ferry raid.

ℱ ℱ ℱ

"Hey Matthew," Owen began.

"Yeah."

"You ever hear of Abraham Lincoln?"

"He's running for president. Lost the Senate race against Douglas."

"Right." Owen looked back at me quizzically. "Did they let you read the newspaper on the plantation?"

I laughed. "Not by a long shot. But I'd only been a slave a short time before being sold for teaching Boy to read. Before that I worked in shipping in Philadelphia."

"Oh. Well, anyway, Lincoln made a speech a few years ago about horse thieves and slavery. Did you hear about it?"

"No."

"Well he was trying to make a point about free Kansas and how anyone who helps Negroes could be prosecuted. He said if a man steals a horse, everybody wants to hang the thief. If, however, a Negro such as yourself, is taken from his family and enslaved, the thief gets paid, the person who enslaves the stolen Negro is protected, and the person who tries to return the Negro to his family is prosecuted."

"Money and self-interest change one's perspective, it seems. So, Owen, do you think Lincoln can resolve the slavery matter when he is elected?"

"I'm not so certain he will be elected. And if he is, he's only one man going against many. And the many have a lot to lose if slavery is abolished."

"He's not alone. We're all on his side. We've just got to stay alive long enough to help when the time comes to speak out."

"Father is determined to do whatever is required to make certain the time to speak out comes as soon as possible."

"Harper's Ferry. I know. That's why we're your prisoners."

"Not exactly prisoners. Father simply needs to know how you know anything about what is to occur. And who else knows what you know. This is Father's life's work – his masterpiece – and he cannot take any chances on failure."

"I understand. But who decides what is or isn't failure or success? I mean, is the loss of a hundred lives considered a success or a failure? What about a thousand lives?" I asked.

Owen thought for a full minute or more before responding.

"You pose a complex question. I think that Father would say a thousand lives lost are not too many if it brings about the end of slavery."

"And what would *you* say, Owen? What price is too high?"

Again Owen became silent.

"I suppose for me, it would depend on who the thousand were. If they were plantation owners and overseers, or slave catchers, or any of the refuse that kidnap free young men such as yourself to sell South, well then a thousand men such as they would be no particular loss.

"If, however, the thousand included me, my father, my brothers, and men like Newby . . .."

Owen's voice trailed as he pondered the possibilities.

"I think, Matthew, that I have sacrificed much for the cause. My little brother Frederick, just three years ago in Kansas, shot dead by a damned Border Ruffian. He was just over twenty-five years of age, with no chance to live a normal life. I have not had a chance for a normal life. And yet, Father is right. How many slaves have not had an opportunity to live an unrestrained life? I honestly do not know what price is too high. I think that in this instance, I must trust Father to make the right decision."

I liked Owen. He was a thinker. Perhaps he could have some influence on his father's final decision. Perhaps things could be different.

We rode in silence for several minutes, both thinking heavy thoughts. I forced myself out of those thoughts to again marvel at the natural beauty around me.

Having lightened my frame of mind, I decided to try to return Owen to a happier state.

"Did you hear the joke about the master, the overseer, the slave, and the abolitionist?" I asked.

Owen glanced at me with a smile. "No, I have not heard that one."

"Okay. The master, the overseer, the slave, and the abolitionist were at the gates of heaven.

"St. Peter first approached the slave and asked of him, 'Why should I let you into heaven?'

"The slave thought for a moment and quietly said, 'Well suh, I always did my work, obeyed the massuh, and loved my family.'

"St. Peter nodded and stepped aside, saying, 'Enter these pearly gates and enjoy the rewards of a virtuous life.'

"St. Peter then approached the overseer and asked of him, 'Why should I let you into heaven?'

"The overseer frowned and said, 'I cain't believe you just let a nigger into heaven. You cain't have niggers and good white folk mixing company like that!'

154

"St. Peter nodded and told the overseer, 'You needn't worry about having to mix with him.'

"Then he pulled a lever and an opening appeared in the cloud on which the overseer was standing. The overseer began falling downward, screaming for help. Just before the opening in the cloud closed, a glint of flame shot up through it.

"The abolitionist and the master looked at each other wide-eyed, and then at St. Peter.

"Next, St. Peter approached the abolitionist and asked of him, 'Why should I let you into heaven?'

"The abolitionist replied, 'I have dedicated my life to easing the suffering of oppressed people, and have no problem mixing with all kinds of people.'

"St. Peter nodded and stepped aside, saying, 'Enter these pearly gates and enjoy the rewards of a virtuous life.'

"Finally, St. Peter approached the master and said to him, 'Why should I let you into heaven?'

"The master took a deep breath, looked St. Peter squarely in the eye, and said, 'As I'm sure you know, I have fathered several children with my slaves and plainly have no problems mixing with anyone. All I want from life is to make my slaves happy.'

"With that, St. Peter nodded and told the master, 'I'm delighted to hear you say that. There will be a party in your honor tonight.'

"The master smiled and gave a sigh of relief. Then St. Peter pulled the lever and waved goodbye to the falling master."

A half beat after I finished, I felt Owen's body begin to shudder with laughter.

"In another time, I think Father would like that one," Owen said, as his guffaw died down. "Do you know any other jokes?"

"Not many. But here's a riddle. How come abolitionists are rarely successful ranchers?"

After a few seconds of thinking, Owen asked, "Why is that?"

I replied, "Well, abolitionists have trouble being ranchers because they keep setting all their livestock free."

Owen smiled and gave a polite chuckle.

"Hey, they can't all be hilarious," I said. "As someone once said, Tennyson I believe, and I paraphrase, 'Tis better to have joked and lost than never to have joked at all.'"

"You are an unusual lad," Owen observed.

"Aye, that I can't deny," I agreed.

We continued on with a lighthearted and peaceful ride, except for the beginnings of saddle sores on my tender, yet firm, young butt. Never thought I'd be able to say that after turning forty.

We stayed on a shady path along the base of a mountain, exiting at a church. I saw a town, which we avoided, instead taking a country road straight to our final destination.

The two-story main house, constructed of stone, brick, and logs, was a good hundred yards or more from the road, distant enough from prying eyes I suppose. Across the road, on what appeared to be swampland, was a smaller, less pleasant log cabin surrounded by plant life. Owen said that the property was known as the Kennedy farm, and that both houses were theirs, but we headed toward the larger place. I later found out we were now a mere five miles from Harper's Ferry.

15

Osawatomie Brown

As we approached the house, two young women came out to greet us. Owen pointed to the younger of the two and said she was Annie, his 15-year-old sister. The other was Martha, wife of his brother Oliver.

As we rode closer, I got a better look at Martha, who appeared to be pregnant. She looked to be in her late teens or early twenties.

I was pleased to see other women, and assumed they too would be pleased to see another woman, but they greeted the others and asked about Boy before turning to me. Then it hit me again that I was a young Black man to everyone except myself. I wondered if at some point my self-perception would change, but I knew I did not want to be here in this time long enough to see that happen.

Owen introduced us to Annie and Martha, and then to Oliver, who came out during the introductions. Oliver was dark-haired and dashing, no more than twenty-one or twenty-two, and built like a farmer with powerful forearms and broad shoulders. He and Owen didn't look much like brothers, and I found out later that they had different mothers.

"Let us enter the house and unburden ourselves," Brown announced. "It is best we not linger and draw attention."

He always talked like that, as if he were a character in a Victorian novel.

Once inside, Annie hugged her father like she thought she'd never see him again, burying her face in his chest while he returned her embrace and kissed her atop the head.

I still remembered the photos and drawings I'd seen of Brown in history classes. In each, he looked like a wild-eyed madman, not just capable of savage acts of violence, but eager to inflict pain. As far as I knew, none of my ancestors enslaved anyone. To me, slavery was an atrocious chapter in the narrative of our country, and especially my home state of Texas. Nonetheless, Brown's use of terror to bring about emancipation had always appalled me. Never, until that moment with Annie, had I imagined another side to him.

"I'm so glad you are safe. I was worried you would not return before Martha and I departed for North Elba, Father," Annie said to Brown.

"You needn't have worried, child. Our Father has work yet for me to do and thus I am protected. And I would not lightly forego the opportunity to bid you and Martha farewell."

Owen gave Annie a quick hug and then took a crew of men outside to unload the wagon. White and Black men seemed to be coming out of the woodwork, from upstairs and the basement to see Brown's return and help with the wagon. I counted at least fifteen that day in the relatively small house.

Brown then asked Martha and Annie to prepare a plate for Boy while he and I spoke in private. He led me to a small neat bedroom, apparently belonging to one or both of the women, and closed the door.

♂ ♂ ♂

"Very few know of our plans. Not even all who reside in this house know everything. Yet, upon meeting me, you, whom I have never met nor heard of before, immediately associate me with Harper's Ferry. How is this?"

"Well, Mr. Brown sir, the story is long, complex, and, quite truthfully, hard to believe."

"I shall be the judge of your story, however fantastic. You appear to have charmed both Owen and Mr. Newby, but I am not easily hornswoggled. Understand that you will be treated accordingly if you are revealed to be a spy," Brown stated in an even tone, definitely threatening, but without malice or extraneous emotion.

Brown motioned for me to sit in a chair in the far corner of the room while he sat on a corner of the bed facing me.

Knowing how absurd the I'm-from-the-future story would sound, I began my story with Matthew's death and revival, explaining that upon awakening, I became a new person. I could now read, I spoke differently, and got occasional detailed visions of the future in my dreams. Bizarre, but not off the scales weird for a man of Brown's faith, I hoped.

I related how I worked with William Still, how he invited me to a meeting of the Vigilance Society, and my introduction to Harriet Tubman.

Brown listened intently, rarely interrupting. He studied me as if discrepancies would show on my face and in my body language.

When I mentioned distracting the hounds while Tubman slept, he gave a slight nod.

"I met with General Tubman in April and we discussed our present venture. I find it hard to believe she would share this information with you, for all intents, a stranger."

"She didn't say anything to me about Harper's Ferry. I know of it through my visions, which began after my revival."

Brown took a moment to consider my story.

"Something does not ring true, albeit what, I cannot say. However, my son, John Jr., met with the General in Boston just weeks ago and she told him of a young man who disappeared while she was asleep during a foray into Maryland. She was to have joined us here, but unfortunately has fallen ill."

I pondered this new information. Harriet had not yet been captured and was now too ill to travel. Thus she could not be hung prior to Harper's Ferry as my history recorded. I changed history!

Apparently Harriet *was* supposed to have been caught during our journey earlier this year. I mistakenly assumed she was captured in the fall just prior to being hung. Instead, in my old timeline, she must have been caught in the spring on the trip that I stumbled into, and then been imprisoned for months before being hung.

I didn't know if this was good or bad, my changing history. I had saved a life – a very important life – but I could conceivably have caused lives to be lost too.

As Spider-Man would say, "With great power comes great responsibility."

I did not want that kind of responsibility.

"Matthew."

Brown's voice snapped me out of my unresolvable musings.

"Matthew. I cannot say I am prepared to fully accept your story, but I find myself curious about what

162

else you may have seen in your visions regarding our future endeavor. How successful will we be?"

Great responsibility. But can I save lives? I decided to tell Brown the truth and hope he saw reason.

"Harper's Ferry went pretty smoothly," I began, recalling what I could from past history courses. "You apparently went in and out like a ghost. However, after you attacked the first plantation and liberated its slaves, things got ugly.

"In response to your freeing of slaves, bands of bounty hunters, so-called southern patriots, and other ne'er-do-wells formed, eventually adopting the name Saviors of the South. At first, the SS tried to apprehend you and your followers to get the bounty, but for most, that proved too dangerous. They decided instead to go after the slaves you had freed. Some were returned alive for rewards, but others were slaughtered.

"In turn, your guerrilla attacks on plantations became more bloody, and over the course of almost two years, well over a thousand people, Black and White, were killed. The Saviors, or bands of ruffians pretending to be Saviors, even began to raid plantations, masquerading as your followers. They kidnapped slaves and killed Whites, in your name, and later returned the slaves for money.

"Finally, the federal government had to step in. Soldiers had minimal success in trying to end your campaign, so Congress began working on what eventually came to be called the Emancipation Compromise.

"The Compromise nearly led to a war between the North and the South, but ultimately the slaveholders realized the institution that made them wealthy could cost them their lives. They agreed to begin paying the slaves a minimal wage and educating the children. Slavery, insofar as the buying and selling of humans, was phased out during Lincoln's second term in office but servitude wasn't completely gone until 1900 when the final stage of the Negro Emancipation Act was concluded. Many older Blacks stayed on the plantations, while the younger ones usually struck out for the West and the North. Most had received some limited education while on the plantation, but still often had to take menial jobs. It took another fifty years before things became more or less equitable between the races."

After I stopped speaking, Brown covered his face with his hands, taking slow, deep breaths. A minute or more passed before he stood and spoke.

"Forty years. And then fifty more. That's too long, Matthew. Your story does not sound outside the realm of possibility. But it is far too long. Think about all of the children like young Boy. They will be old men and women before they truly taste freedom. All those years lost, wasted."

"And all those lives lost, Mr. Brown. There must be a better way," I said.

164

Brown slowly paced the small room.

"Yes, a better way. But it eludes me. I must pray. You and Boy must stay indoors until this thing is done."

"But, why? Why must this thing be done, sir?"

Brown looked at me, and then beyond me.

"When I was twelve, my father entrusted me with considerable responsibility. On one occasion, I drove a herd of cattle one hundred miles across Ohio, alone, to a quartermaster depot.

"I stayed for a short time with a gentleman who owned a slave boy of about my age. The boy was forced to live in the cold, poorly clothed and fed. Worse still, the gentleman beat the child with iron shovels or anything else that was convenient. I could not make sense of such cruelty. Have not you too experienced unreasonable mistreatment at the hands of a master or overseer?"

He regarded me with a damp-eyed, weight-of-the-world stare.

"Man's inhumanity to man. That is why I must do what I do."

16

Life on the Farm

Meal preparation took place in the living room at a wood-burning stove. Upon touring the house, I found a proper kitchen in the basement, but it was stuffed with supplies such as blankets, clothing, boots, food, dozens of Sharps rifles, revolvers, ammunition, and hundreds of Collinsville pikes.

I had never seen a pike before. It looked like a martial arts style weapon, with a sharp, double-edged blade affixed to a long pole. Owen said that it was a good weapon in close quarters fighting, but unpleasant to use. I shuddered to think how desperate one would have to be to stab and hack at another human being with such a cruel looking implement.

In different rooms throughout the house, men were cleaning weapons, doing leatherwork, playing cards or checkers, talking, reading, or writing. The young women and Boy seemed to light up whatever area they entered just by smiling or waving or saying a quick hello.

Conversely, when Brown passed, the mood immediately became more serious. Though no one actually stood and saluted, it was clear that almost to a man, their posture changed as if they were internally standing at attention.

Pallets were set up for Boy and me in the crowded basement. Though it was never stated outright, forcing us to negotiate the gauntlet of men and supplies to exit the house was intentional. After witnessing Brown and his men efficiently and dispassionately dispatch the three highwaymen just two days ago, it seemed wise not to test them.

After dinner on our second night at the farm, Boy and I went outside with Owen, Annie, and Dangerfield Newby. Newby, I think, reminded Boy of his father, and Boy must have reminded Newby of his children. While the two of them explored the area, Owen, Annie, and I sat on the steps on the side of the farmhouse.

"Father is going away again," said Annie. "Martha and I are to meet him at the Harrisburg depot on Thursday. Oliver will take us."

"Although I've not gotten to know you well, I'll miss you both," I said to Annie.

"And I you," Annie replied. "You are different from most boys. You act older than you look, and treat Boy as your ward."

"He is. I promised his father I would reunite them. And somehow, I will."

"Unless Newby decides to adopt you both," Owen joked.

"Ha. I suspect Newby's wife would object to him adding two more to their clan of seven," I said.

"Maybe Annie could adopt you when she marries Will," Owen teased, putting his hands over his heart.

"Or Albert," I added.

In my limited time around Brown's recruits, I'd observed that Will Leeman, while closest in age to Annie, was too rowdy and unsettled for her. Albert Hazlett was both cuter and more easy-going.

"Shush, the both of you. As much as I care about our cause, I shall marry a man who will stay closer to home. Mother has too much to bear alone, and I would not like to share her circumstance, always waiting in North Elba for Father to return or to receive news of his demise."

"Well spoken, sister. I would suggest staying away from Stewart then. I hear he has already written his last will and testament."

"I have heard the same," Annie said. "He has spoken to me of other worlds and his own death. I would definitely prefer someone cheerier."

I nodded my agreement. Though I'd never spoken with Stewart Taylor, every time I saw him, he seemed a detached observer, going about tasks almost robotically.

"How about Dauphin?" I suggested. "He's handsome and young. Maybe you could convince him to leave with you and Martha."

"Father would forbid it. And I'm in no hurry to marry. You will marry before I. And Owen too. Somewhere there must be a woman desperate enough to marry my oaf of a brother. Perhaps a woman from one of Stewart's ethereal worlds."

"Thank you dear sister for those words of discouragement. You have no idea how much I'll miss your gay countenance," Owen deadpanned, and then looked at me holding two fingers a centimeter apart.

"More seriously, Owen," Annie said, "you must now run interference with Mrs. Huffmaster and her brood."

Facing me, she explained, "Our neighbor, one shoeless Mrs. Huffmaster, has made it a habit to come by unannounced with her four ragamuffins. On more than one occasion I've had to convince her that we are not harboring runaways. She usually becomes more at ease with the situation after I offer a small gift."

"Perhaps I'll invite her over for high tea and crumpets," Owen suggested with a straight face as he pantomimed holding a teacup with his pinkie outstretched.

"That sounds positively divine!" I interjected, smiling at Owen with a semi-straight face.

"You two clowns!" Annie chided, trying to suppress a giggle. "I suspect things will fall apart when Martha and I depart. Any tea party the two of you endeavor to coordinate should no doubt turn out like the one in Boston some eighty years ago."

Owen and I looked at each other for a second and then nodded in agreement, bursting into laughter.

We continued talking and joking for another hour. Though it was never spoken, I could tell Owen and Annie were trying to enjoy each other's company for what could well be the final time.

The funny thing about my situation was that although I had been a teenaged Black male in the 1850s for over a year, I still felt like a 40-year-old White female from the 1990s. Almost every day I caught myself about to make an inappropriate remark for someone of my new age or sex or race.

Other than George and Oleta, I felt most comfortable talking with Owen and Annie. I couldn't sense any judgment or unease coming from them when I spoke, as I could with most other people, Black or White. They were truly at ease talking with and relating to Blacks. Had it not been for his suspicions (altogether justified) regarding me, Brown and I might have also made a connection.

⅏ ⅏ ⅏

170

On Thursday, September 29, Annie and the visibly pregnant Martha climbed into the back of a mule-drawn wagon to leave the house to us men. Martha's husband, Oliver Brown, rode up front with his older brother Watson. I had almost no contact with the tall, serious Watson on the farm. He always seemed focused on whatever task was at hand, unlike Owen who always had time for a laugh.

John Brown, who had been away on a recruitment and fundraising mission in Philadelphia, was to meet them in Harrisburg and then return with Watson. Oliver would accompany his young wife and Annie from the Harrisburg depot as far as Troy, New York before coming back to the Kennedy farm.

Maybe I watched too much TV, but I expected tearful goodbyes. Instead, everyone was remarkably stoic. Owen and I hugged Annie and Martha, with Annie whispering to me to watch over her father and brothers.

I was glad that the women wouldn't be around for the forthcoming violence and mayhem. At the same time, I wished Boy and I didn't have to be around for it either.

"I think Boy should go with you," I said to the Browns, suddenly inspired. "He could, I don't know, maybe pretend to be your servant. He shouldn't be here."

"Father said you were not to leave," Oliver said sternly.

"I will stay, but this business ahead of us is not for a child. You know that."

"He makes a good point," Owen interjected. "Father would want the child to grow up free."

"I only ask that you watch him until I'm free to leave. Or better yet, you could leave him with my parents in Philadelphia. I'll write a note explaining the situation to them. Please?"

Brothers Owen, Oliver, and Watson conferred with one another solely by making eye contact. Owen nodded first, followed by Watson and a somewhat reluctant Oliver.

"We'll have to figure out how to get him by the patrols, but I agree that Father would approve," Watson added.

I ran inside to tell Boy and write an explanatory note. He had nothing to pack, so physically, he was ready. I put my hands on his shoulders and told him my plan.

"Remember I told you about my parents and my little sister? You're going to go stay with them until I can get back."

"What about Daddy and Paula?" he asked.

"Once I get back to Philadelphia, we'll come up with a plan to get them. Okay?"

"Okay," he agreed trustingly.

172

As we exited the house, Dangerfield called out, "Hold up. I got something for the boy."

He was inside for a minute and came out with a clean, white button-down shirt in his hands, just about the perfect size for Boy. It must have been purchased as a gift for one of his kids.

"Put this on, fella. White folks usually like they servants to look good, I guess cause it makes them look like good masters. I know you got comfortable around these folks since you been here, but when you around other people, it's best to look any place but right at White folk. Just like when you was on the plantation. Can you remember that?"

Boy looked up at Dangerfield adoringly, and said quite seriously, "Yah suh."

Then, looking at Annie, Martha, Watson, and Oliver, Dangerfield advised them, "Don't talk to him like a person when other people is around. And he always needs to look like he doing something, even if it's just carrying a bag. Won't hurt if you cuff him if it look like somebody getting suspicious. It won't hurt him near as much as being sent back to the plantation."

They all listened closely and nodded.

As uncomfortable as I was with Boy's name, I couldn't help but think how fortuitous it was in case the women were overheard addressing him.

I gave Boy a long hug and whispered that I would see him soon.

And then they were gone.

♂ ♂ ♂

When Brown returned to the farm, he reported that he had not heard from Frederick Douglass and his announcement caused an immediate depression throughout the house.

Owen later explained that Brown had met with Douglass in Philadelphia in August, but Douglass had at that time refused to join the raid. Shields Green, a fugitive slave who had accompanied Douglass to Philadelphia, did come to the cause and was already on the farm awaiting the next step. During this most recent trip, Brown had hoped for word that Douglass had a change of heart, and was devastated that he did not have Douglass' support.

Later that evening, Brown took me aside again.

"How do you explain to someone a thing which should be as apparent as the nose on his face? Water is wet. The sun is bright. People should be free. We have a responsibility to help, for if not us, then who?"

I took the questions to be rhetorical and just stood there quietly, wondering how I would answer if I could.

Brown continued.

"I did my best to impart to Mr. Douglass how well the Allegheny Mountains are suited to our purpose. With only twenty or so men, we could use the Alleghenies as a base to end slavery in a short time. As much as I want to think the best of Mr. Douglass, I can only conclude that he fears death. And perhaps he can better serve our cause in another way."

Brown then fixed his piercing eyes on mine and asked, "What happens to me? In your visions, I mean. I did not wish to know before and may regret knowing once told, but at this moment I require ... something. Do I live to see my Mary again?"

I had been trying for days to recall everything I'd ever studied about Brown and Harper's Ferry and its aftermath. Though I'd hoped he'd never ask, I answered truthfully.

"Two days into the forays, people began claiming to have killed you. Yet others claimed to have seen you lead raids for years afterwards. It was a mystery until 1900, when one of your sons finally revealed that you were mortally wounded and died during the first year of your campaign. They decided it would be best for the cause if one of them masqueraded as you to maintain morale and enthusiasm among your supporters, and to preserve the element of fear among the slaveholders."

Brown hung his head and sighed.

After a long pause, he looked at me again and said, "Thank you, Matthew. I know that if I do nothing, then nothing will be done. If I do what I have planned, not enough will be done. I am beginning to grasp what the Lord requires of me."

Although I'm not sure what I could have done, I wish I'd comprehended the meaning of Brown's cryptic words.

፠ ፠ ፠

The uneasy mood at the farm intensified, in part due to a lack of money for supplies and the discomfort of living in such close quarters. When the news came that a slave from a nearby farm had hung himself in the Kennedy orchard after his wife had been sold away from him, agitation levels in the house increased even more. The men were ready for action, but Brown was hesitant to proceed for some reason.

Dangerfield Newby would sometimes leave the farm to hire himself out as a laborer. That allowed him to tap into the news and gossip of the area. His announcement that a warrant was being sought to search the farm buildings further heightened what was already a tense situation. Newby found out that neighbors had seen the wagon make so many trips that they suspected the farm was being used to either run stolen guns or help fugitive slaves.

Clearly, Brown would have to make a decision soon.

On Saturday, October 15, an odd, slender, pale young man with dark hair and only one eye named Francis Merriam arrived on the farm. Unlike the other men at the farm, he did not seem at all battle-hardened, rugged, or macho, nor did he seem particularly bright. Definitely not someone to inspire confidence in a combat situation.

His sole constructive attribute, other than his general enthusiasm, was the $250 he brought with him to

176

contribute to the cause along with primers, percussion caps, and ammo.

Two other men, both Black, also arrived that day. John Copeland, who was an Oberlin College student, and his uncle, Lewis Leary, a leatherworker and saddler, had been recruited earlier in the year. Unlike Merriam, Copeland and Leary were already active in the antislavery cause. Just the year before, they had helped rescue a Black man in Ohio from deputies who had kidnapped the man and were attempting to return him to slavery under the Fugitive Slave Act.

Despite the admirable resumes of Copeland and Leary, Francis Merriam and his money are what seemed to prompt Brown to announce that on the next night, the revolution would begin.

17

Pretzel Logic

I'd been selfishly looking forward to this day since I arrived on the farm. Brown had promised to release me once the assault was under way.

Not counting me, there were 22 men at the farmhouse. I was to stay behind there with Owen, Merriam, and Barclay Coppoc while the others went with Brown on the raid. When the time came, Owen's job would be to transport guns and pikes to a schoolhouse on the Potomac River for arming slaves from Maryland, as well as Whites from southern Pennsylvania and western Virginia who would ideally be inspired to participate in the revolution. Once we'd taken the weapons to the schoolhouse, I'd be free to work my way back to Philly.

Final preparations for the assault began Sunday morning after a fervent Bible reading by Brown about the duty of others to free those in bondage. To a man, we were all rapt, absorbing his words, and feeling inspired by both the message and the delivery. In my case, though, not inspired enough to follow a well-intentioned, but possibly mad man on a killing spree.

Next, Aaron Stevens, who acted as Brown's second in command and who usually led the military drills in the farmhouse, read the Provisional Constitution of the Chatham Convention. Owen had previously explained to me that in May of last year, a constitutional convention had been convened in Chatham, Ontario to condemn slavery, and that it, in a way, laid the groundwork for Harper's Ferry.

All 48 articles of the Provisional Constitution were read aloud. Despite Stevens' serious tone and imposing physical presence, the lengthy recitation caused some of us to fidget like schoolchildren, most especially the naturally hyper Francis Merriam who paced like an expectant father, nodding and whispering, "Yes" after each article was recited.

Lastly, Brown gave the oath of secrecy to the recent arrivals, Merriam, Copeland, and Leary. Once they agreed, he explained to them the strategy of blocking off the two bridges that accessed Harper's Ferry prior to securing the armory. Hostages would serve to discourage attacks.

As the time drew nearer to depart, Brown, in a somber tone, told the men, "Do not spill blood needlessly, but do not hesitate in defending yourselves either." He looked each man in the eye as they nodded their assent.

At eight o'clock that evening, Brown announced, "Men, get on your arms. We will proceed to the Ferry." He pulled on an old cap with the earflaps down and climbed into a wagon loaded with pikes, and other tools and weapons.

Just when it appeared he would drive off into the near moonless, misty night with the other eighteen men who were marching on foot for the five-mile journey to Harper's Ferry, Brown called me to him.

Looking down at me from the wagon, he said, "I know that you have great courage, Matthew. When first we met, you were engaged in combat with three unsavory sorts intent on stealing you and the boy away from still another less than savory gentleman. I believe it is God's plan for you to accompany us this evening."

"I'm, uh, perfectly fine with staying here, sir," I said, my nervousness at the idea plain in my voice.

"Do not fear God's plan. You are part of that plan and I shall make certain no harm comes to you. Please. Come."

Brown fixed me yet again with his piercing steel-gray eyes and I appeared beside him on the wagon's bench seat without recalling exactly how I got there, as if not of my own volition.

"I will not kill," I stated resolutely. "Bloodshed is not necessary. Reasonable people should be able to resolve this matter without resorting to shooting and chopping each other up."

"Reasonable men should, young Matthew, but you would need to look long and far to find such men down here in Africa. Those who embrace the peculiar institution clearly do not also embrace reason."

I sat silent, recognizing a good point when I heard it. However, I also knew how gruesome Brown's mission would be.

Brown shook the reins, made a clucking sound at the horses, and we proceeded out of the driveway and onto the dirt road leading to Harper's Ferry.

Charles Tidd and John Cook walked in front of the wagon with the remaining men following the wagon, marching in pairs. The two men leading the procession usually hung out together at the house when Cook, who had a job in Harper's Ferry, visited. I'd had minimal contact with either of them, but I got the impression that Cook was a spy for the cause. When he stopped in, he was quick with a story or gossip from his time in town.

I buttoned my shabby, hand-me-down jacket and pulled my old wide-brimmed work hat tight against my head. Then I took my thin, rough leather gloves out of the jacket pockets and tugged them on to retain whatever heat there was in my body, figuring it wouldn't get any warmer during the night.

Our journey was so calm and quiet that I actually nodded off for brief periods, lulled by the metronomic clopping of the horse's hooves and the wagon's rattles and moans. At one point, Stevens clambered up beside me on the bench seat to confer with Brown so I moved to the bed of the wagon and dozed for most of the remaining ride.

A train whistle awakened me as we approached the town from above. Brown told me we were on Maryland Heights and pointed out the Potomac River below us where the railroad bridge crossed. I'd heard the choppy waters of the river to our right as we descended southward from the farm, but at the base of the hill, the waterway's course turned and ran more or less east-west.

South of the railroad bridge was the Shenandoah River. It ran from the southwest to the northeast and converged with the Potomac near the railroad bridge at an acute angle. A second covered bridge spanned the Shenandoah River not far below the train bridge.

Finally, to our right and just across the train bridge between the two rivers was Harper's Ferry itself, in the state of Virginia. The town began at a point and widened to the west between the rivers as the two bodies of water diverged.

I'd guess it to have been ten or eleven o'clock by then, but even in the dim light of a somewhat foggy night, the view was spectacular.

As we drew closer to the bridge, Brown called a halt to our procession. The men, who had discreetly kept their weapons out of view or in the wagon bed, first shifted their ammunition to more accessible locations outside of their coats. Next, they gripped their weapons, to now look like the formidable raiders they actually were.

Brown then motioned to Tidd and Cook with his hand. They took off double time ahead of us to the bridge spanning the Potomac River.

Large rocks jutted up out of the Potomac in places, along with narrow islets. Had the river not been so wide, it probably would not have been navigable at all with so many obstacles.

While I was appreciating the natural beauty, Tidd shinnied up a telegraph pole and cut the wires. Then John Henry Kagi and Aaron Stevens entered the pedestrian path alongside the train tracks on the covered bridge and disappeared from sight into the darkness.

Brown directed his son Watson, along with Stewart Taylor, to guard the bridge on the Maryland side while the rest of us crossed. By the time we reached the other side of the bridge, Kagi had a night watchman in custody and Stevens' rifle was pressed against the chest of another guard at the entrance to the Armory.

It had begun.

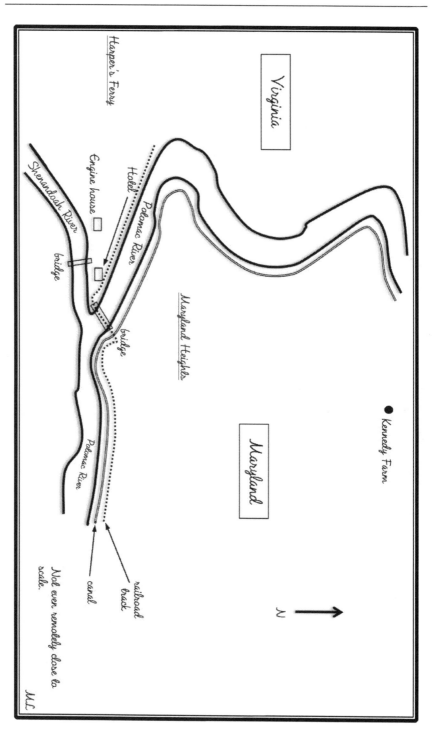

Virginia

Harper's Ferry

Engine house

Shenandoah River

Hotel

Potomac River

bridge

bridge

Maryland Heights

Kennedy Farm

Maryland

Potomac River

canal

railroad track

Not even remotely close to scale.

N

ML

18

The Prince of Beall-Air

The guard being held at gunpoint was shaking with fear. Yet when Stevens ordered him to either open the Armory gate or relinquish the keys, the brave man refused. Brave, or foolhardy, he was ultimately lucky.

Instead of punishing the guard, Brown's men simply grabbed crowbars out of the wagon and forced the lock open.

Brown sent his son Oliver with William Thompson to watch over the bridge across the Shenandoah River, and directed John Copeland and Kagi to the Rifle Works up the street that ran parallel to the Shenandoah River.

Across the street from the Armory was a structure Brown referred to as the Arsenal. He assigned Albert

Hazlett and Edwin Coppoc to guard it, while the rest of us stayed at the Armory.

"Captain," Brown said to Aaron Stevens, "take your men now. Don't forget the sword and the pistol. And take young Matthew with you. Perhaps when he sees how his brethren respond to freedom, he will better understand our mission."

"Not necessary," I protested. "As I've said, I understand fully, but disagree with the method."

"No time to waste," Stevens snapped. "Come."

I followed, if only to get away from what I knew to be the focal point of the raid. Cook, Tidd, Osborne Anderson, Lewis Leary, and Shields Green were the other members of our party.

We left on foot southward, toward Charlestown according to the signage. Stevens set a much faster pace than the walk from the farm earlier, but we were all young and kept up.

Although Stevens was abrupt with me that night, we'd actually had a couple of weighty, but absorbing and illuminating conversations as part of a larger group while holed up at the farm.

Several weeks before the raid, Stevens, Brown and several others were, as was their wont, discussing religion. I expected them all to be on the same page, but while Brown was a devout Calvinist, even his own sons differed with him regarding religion. Owen Brown went so far as to declare himself to be agnostic, as did Kagi. Stewart

Taylor, who was stationed back at the railroad bridge, considered himself a spiritualist, and calmly predicted that his days were nearing an end.

Stevens was an odd mix, saying he believed there must be a higher being, yet he rejected Christianity and organized religion in general. Paradoxically, he would quote from Thomas Paine's *The Age of Reason*, yet express a belief in séances and the dead communicating by spirit rapping.

Perhaps because I was in bondage when they met me, Stevens and some of the others who had not yet interacted with me seemed to assume I was an uneducated, career slave. It would be a perfectly natural assumption considering my vintage, plantation chic wardrobe and the circumstances under which I was first encountered.

During the group conversation, however, I chimed in to proclaim my agnosticism and agree with Stevens about organized religion. In all likelihood, I'd had more experience with life after death than anyone else in the house, but I still essentially had no real knowledge about any higher being or what happens long-term after death.

Stevens' eyes lit up when I made my declaration, and later, he smiled when I challenged his assertion that spirits of the dead talk to us.

No matter the different religious beliefs of the group, they all found common ground on slavery.

♪ ♪ ♪

Stevens was the true soldier of the group and he had a laser focus now that the mission was under way.

"How can you not be in favor of our mission?" Stevens asked me as we hiked briskly through the dark, our way lit by the large wooden torch he carried.

"A part of me would love to put a gun to the head of the man who carved permanent grooves into my back with a whip," I admitted, "and also the man who ordered it. However, I want to rise above their level and be civilized. I'm not ready to kill."

"That would be my first choice too, Matthew, but experience has shown me that reason, logic, and appeals to human decency don't work. And the South *is* willing to kill to maintain their way of life."

I considered what Stevens said and wondered if I could be wrong. I was still a relative newcomer to this time. My interactions had been limited. However, I had no reason to disbelieve the history books I had grown up reading. A compromise would be reached.

We continued in silence, finally stopping in front of a large, two-story stuccoed brick mansion with four white columns supporting the roof of the covered porch.

Stevens ordered Leary and Green to stand watch outside while the rest of us approached the rear door. Cook, who was armed to the teeth with two revolvers, a rifle, and a Bowie knife, knocked on the door as if we were expected for afternoon tea. No one answered so he knocked again.

Leary said women were looking out of the upstairs windows. Still, no one came to the door.

Stevens shrugged and then tried the door handle. It was unlocked so we followed him inside. With weapons in hand, Stevens, Cook, Anderson, and Tidd began searching for the plantation owner, while I stayed near the door, unsure of what to do with myself.

After a minute, I heard another door open, followed by voices, toward the front of the house. I eased down the hallway to get a better look and hear what was being said. At the far end of the hallway, two women in robes huddled together in fear.

A tall, balding, mustachioed man in slippers and a nightshirt was telling Stevens, "You can take the slaves, if you allow me to stay here at Beall-Air." Despite his attire, the man stood firm with his shoulders back and chest out.

Stevens simply told the man, "No. You must come with us. Get dressed." He then exited the house, leaving Cook, Tidd, and Anderson to guard the man that I assumed to be the plantation owner.

"Who is that man?" I quietly asked Anderson, assuming the Black man would be more likely to answer me.

"That," Anderson whispered to me conspiratorially, "is Colonel Lewis Washington, the great-grandnephew of President George Washington."

190

19

Prisoners, Hostages, and Casualties

Voilà! That explained why Brown was so keen on that particular hostage.

Despite having met Harriet Tubman and John Brown, I was still blown away by the fact that a few people who were alive when Washington was president still walked the earth. His kinsmen were likely looked upon as something near royalty.

Colonel Lewis Washington dressed nervously and then led us into the dining room to wait, saying it should be warmer in there.

When Stevens returned, Washington, ever the genteel lord of the manor, asked, "Would any of you care for a drink?" Who observes social niceties with armed invaders?

Stevens, ever the steadfast soldier, politely refused, as did the other armed raiders, so the Colonel drank alone. I stayed in the background as much as I could, silently observing the awkward, impromptu cocktail party. However, I wouldn't have said no to hors d'oeuvres or petits fours if proffered.

Stevens next demanded all of the man's weapons, specifically mentioning the pistol given to General George Washington by Lafayette and a sword given to him by Frederick the Great of Prussia. I could tell by his body language that Colonel Washington wanted to protest, but after a quick glance at Stevens, Cook, Anderson, and Tidd, he relented and began gathering what was requested.

Stevens took a double-barreled shotgun, a rifle, and two large flintlock pistols when Washington handed them over, but insisted Washington present the historic sword to a Black man, Osborne Anderson.

This gesture, though, was apparently too much for Washington who openly balked, saying, "You ask too much, sir."

Washington and Stevens began a staring contest, which ended abruptly after Cook and Tidd raised their rifles. Anderson approached the Colonel who reluctantly handed over the sword, avoiding eye contact with the Black man. Anderson, however, understood the symbolism of the moment, and nodded politely to Washington anyway as he accepted the weapon.

192

I'd spoken a bit with Anderson at the farm and liked him. He was a quiet, sober guy, but when he spoke, it was clear he was educated. Anderson told me he was born free in Pennsylvania, but worked in Canada as a printer prior to joining Brown's ranks.

Washington and a Black house servant were hustled outside and onto a fancy carriage with Cook and Tidd. The rest of Washington's male slaves were ordered into the back of a huge four-horse wagon, which must have been liberated from Washington's barn.

We headed back into the darkness the way we had come, Stevens driving the larger wagon with Lewis Leary seated beside him. Anderson, Shields Green, and I rode in the back of the clattering conveyance with Washington's slaves.

I was uncertain as to whether my place was with the prisoners or the kidnappers. Since no one spoke, perhaps they too were uncertain.

We stopped three times while en route back to Harper's Ferry.

The first stop was simply to reposition the horses, which had become difficult to manage. When Brown's men first harnessed the animals, they unknowingly put one of the lead horses in the wrong position, altering the chemistry of the team.

Next, we stopped at a private home. I assumed they would take more prisoners, but after conversations at the front door and the carriage, we continued onward.

The third stop was considerably more involved.

Upon our arrival at another stately home, Cook knocked on the front door. From my position in the rear of the large wagon, I could not hear what was said, but the door was not opened. Stevens, Tidd, and Cook immediately hurried off the porch to a split-rail fence and removed one of the heavy wooden rails. Then they used the rail as a battering ram and stormed into the house.

Almost immediately, a window opened, and a woman, probably young from the sound of the voice, screamed, "Murder!"

My companions in the wagon looked at one another and rolled their eyes at her premature proclamation. Since no gunshots had been fired, I assumed her cry was simply the 19th century version of calling 911. The only murder that could have happened that quickly would have the door itself as the victim.

Another loud bashing sound emanated from the house, and several minutes later, two clearly cowed White men, one younger and the other older, were hustled out to the wagon and onto the bench seat. I later learned they were a father and son, John and John Thomas Allstadt.

Anderson and Green then went to the slave quarters and returned with six more male slaves who were crowded into the large wagon with me and Washington's slaves. The two sets of slaves seemed to have at least a nodding acquaintance, but they remained quiet, waiting to see how it all played out.

When we again hit the road, Anderson, Green, Leary, and Tidd were on foot, pacing the carriage and the now jam-packed wagon. We made quick time back to the Armory gates.

Brown had set up headquarters of a sort in a building they referred to as the engine house, which held firefighting equipment. It was a brick structure with two sets of tall, double doors, and a third regular door on the left. They called the office area behind the single doorway the watch house.

Everyone from both the wagon and carriage was hustled into either the engine house area or the watch house. I could see Brown himself greet and speak with Washington, but again could not hear what was being said. A short time later, Washington joined us in the watch house.

When the slaves were offered pikes from Brown's wagon to arm themselves, most took the vicious looking spears with no enthusiasm, unsure of what might happen next.

I again refused weaponry and was sent back into the watch house as if I were one of Washington or Allstadt's slaves. Neither Brown nor any of the other raiders acknowledged me as an acquaintance. I didn't understand it at the time, thinking Brown was angry with me.

Brown ordered Cook and Tidd to drive Washington's large wagon back to the farm to help Owen and the others that were left behind to load more supplies and weapons. Some slaves were sent with them, but I couldn't tell how many. I wanted to ask to join the group going back, but before I could decide how to approach a possibly irate Brown, the wagon had left.

Daybreak was upon us, but it was still somewhat dark and the watch house was warm, so I settled in next to the pot-bellied stove, hoping to grab a few more minutes of sleep. One lesson that I learned as a slave was to sleep when I could. A bit of extra energy might be needed on any given day.

My eyes were barely shut when I heard a gunshot. Everyone in the room, slaves and slaveholders, rushed toward the windows and door, curiosity outweighing fear for the moment.

When a second blast rang out seconds later, though, we all either flattened ourselves against the walls or the floor. The bravest of us waited a few seconds to see if any more shooting would occur, and then continued to the windows to see what was happening.

Smoke still curled from the barrel of the Sharps rifle of my friend Dangerfield Newby, Boy's surrogate father while he was at Brown's rented farm. Dangerfield was on one knee, scoping the area. A large White man lay in the street with blood flowing from his lower abdomen and a gun by his side.

It was easy to figure out what happened, knowing the kind of man Dangerfield was. The wounded man fired at Dangerfield and missed. Dangerfield returned fire and did not.

That moment served as a graphic reminder and a wakeup call that I needed to extricate myself from this hairy situation sooner rather than later. The details of the raid were not the focus of the history I had studied, so I had no idea how bad things might get. I'd always assumed the worst of it was after Harper's Ferry, once the raiders had taken refuge in the hills and begun the guerilla attacks on plantations.

This could quickly escalate into a bloodbath if more townspeople decided to take up arms. The whole situation was beginning to feel wrong, and not just in the moral sense.

20

Room Service

In the next hours, an already unreal situation snow-balled into a positively surreal debacle.

Townspeople apparently got word of the situation and did in fact arm themselves. Occasionally, one would fire upon the engine house and Brown's raiders would fire back.

Then, around eight o'clock, Brown made the peculiar move of allowing a few hostages to go home for breakfast. He even sent one of his prisoners to the Wager House Hotel, located just outside the gates of the Armory near the railroad track, to order breakfast for the rest of us.

Incredibly, less than an hour later, after some appar-ent parleying out of my earshot, a young Black man wheeled a pushcart through the gates of the Armory.

Prisoners and raiders alike feasted on ham, hot cakes, eggs, potatoes, and coffee. No decaf, but who's complaining?

Washington, Brown, and Allstadt chose not to partake, however.

"You should eat something," I said to Washington, who sat on the floor near the pot-bellied stove across the small room from me. "You never know when the next chance to eat will come."

He was a tall man and sat with his arms hugging his knees. He looked up at me as he began to respond, a sour expression on his face.

"I know not what may be in the food or coffee. It may be drugged for the purpose of saving a guard over you."

"I hadn't considered that," I said as I chewed, "but since I've already wolfed down several bites, I may as well continue. In for a penny, in for a pound."

He nodded.

"Are you one of Mr. Allstadt's boys?"

Boy? Sure, technically, I was a boy, but I was offended nonetheless and replied accordingly to the great-grandnephew of President George Washington.

"No, I'm no one's *boy*. I was born free. Opportunistic scoundrels kidnapped me and sold me South."

I deliberately left out the exact circumstances of my capture, knowing it would ruin my point and mitigate my right to outrage.

"I cannot condone that, but this, this entire affair is an atrocity."

"I don't agree with the action being taken here either, but neither do I believe in the inhumane, barbaric policy of human bondage.   That is the true atrocity . . . sir."

Washington frowned.

"You must understand that slaves are property and no one can deprive another of his property."

"Really?   Can you debate the issue of property with a cow or a plow or a barn?   If the situation were flipped, would you readily agree to be another's property?   Your position is illogical, and to be blunt, self-serving."

While I was speaking, Washington's expression morphed from annoyance to amusement.

"You, young man, are clearly not a product of one of our fine southern plantations.   I reluctantly cede round one of this debate to you.   However, our economy is based on this system that our captor wishes to eradicate. My fellow Southerners and I will not give it up without a fight."

"I wish to believe that at some point soon, calmer heads will prevail and an agreement can be reached to end the institution over time.   Ideally, with no lives lost in the process."

"What is your name, young man?"

"Matthew."

"Well, Matthew, your idea may be overly optimistic. After over two hundred years, our system of slave labor is firmly ingrained. Any such a proposal would go against the natural order, as we see it. Moreover, it would take money from our pockets. Many would rather die first, although I am not one of that number."

"I hope that won't be the case," I said somberly.

He nodded at that.

I finished stuffing my face in silence, trying to think ahead. My plan was simple. One, escape. Two, get back to Philly.

Now that I had a full stomach, I was ready to look for an opening. I figured we couldn't be staying in town much longer. I'd actually expected the entire raid to be more of an in-and-out operation. A catered breakfast did not fit at all with my recollection of the incident.

⁜ ⁜ ⁜

For the entire time I resided in Brown's house, I made only two enemies.

As I mentioned earlier, Brown's spy in Harper's Ferry, John Cook, stopped by periodically. The first time I saw him, he was regaling a group of men with a tale describing his intimate relations with a young woman from the town.

Cook himself was a short, slender man with blue eyes and blond, curly hair. He was always the best dressed among the group and the most gregarious. I could see how some might find him handsome and charming, but his crass attitude about women rubbed me the wrong way.

I suppose I couldn't hide my distaste as I turned on my heels and stalked away mid-story. Apparently, Cook noticed and word got around that he didn't trust me.

My other enemy was Shields Green, nicknamed Emperor. Green, an escaped former slave, was especially protective of "the old man," as he more often than not referred to Brown.

After my first private conversation with Brown in the house, Brown was visibly upset. Green immediately picked up on that and logically attributed Brown's perturbation to me. From that point on, Green gave me the stink eye whenever he had the opportunity.

Fortunately for me, Brown had sent Cook back to the farm with the large wagon to assist Owen. Unfortunately, Emperor regularly traveled back and forth between the watch house and the engine house, each time eyeing me as if I were a fox in the hen house, a saboteur to the enterprise.

During one such trip, Emperor began escorting the high value hostages, such as Washington, to the engine house. Although the distance was less than ten feet from door to door, the journey was fraught with danger.

After the hotel staff retrieved our breakfast dishes, the townspeople had again begun shooting at our building intermittently. Clearly, the informal ceasefire had come to a close.

Being the prudent sort, I decided to temporarily postpone my escape until the odds of not being riddled with lead were more in my favor.

21

Monday, Bloody Monday

I crept to the door of the watch house, peering out of the small window to the right. Muzzle flashes and puffs of smoke were visible from attic windows and steeples. The corner in which I was situated seemed relatively safe, with solid brick on two sides. Only a shot fired from an extreme angle or a ricochet would reach me. Nonetheless, my fear factor was increasing, so I crouched to make myself a smaller target.

As I mentioned, this would have been a bad time to attempt an escape, even though the shooters at this point were not especially accurate. I did, however, need to come up with an exit strategy for when the time came. The windows at the rear of the watch house were too high to easily climb out of, and the side windows, while large, were too exposed. Be that as it may, at some point, I would have to make an opportunity.

About thirty minutes into the fitful barrage, the glass from the window to the left of the door was shattered. At least one shooter was now finding the broad side of the barn, so to speak. Through the broken window, the sounds of gunfire and shouting voices became clearer. The more distant gunfire reminded me of large fireworks displays on the fourth of July, popping in the distance. The blasts from the Sharps rifles of Brown's men next door were crisper and more like the sounds I was accustomed to from the firing range when I was a police officer.

Brown could just be heard shouting, "Don't waste your powder and shot! Take aim, and make every shot count!"

The call and response gunfire continued through the morning and into the afternoon. Then, in the early afternoon, I heard someone shout, "Troops!" and I knew what was already ugly would soon get uglier.

I just didn't know how ugly.

I hazarded a glance out of the window. Oliver Brown, William Thompson, and Dangerfield Newby were racing across an open area toward the engine house from the direction of the hotel and bridge.

In a flash, a musket fired and Dangerfield fell to the cobblestone pavement, bleeding from his side. I wanted to turn away in horror, but could not.

He rolled over with his weapon, attempting to return fire. Before he could, a second musket blasted a sickeningly accurate round to Dangerfield's head, instantly killing the man who had been so loving with Boy.

My nemesis, Emperor, wailed, and at least eight quick shots boomed from just outside the engine house before its doors were closed again. I could not tell if they hit anyone, but they were clearly frustrated because Dangerfield was too far away for them to try to retrieve his body.

I slumped back to the floor, fought the urge to vomit, and cried softly for my friend. Emotions came in single file, one after the other. First, shock, followed by sadness, hopelessness, helplessness, and finally anger.

What the hell was going on? Who launches a wave of terror from a defensive position? By this time, they should have been hiding in the hills or raiding plantations, freeing slaves and slaughtering owners and overseers.

Instead, Brown and his men were essentially loitering about Harper's Ferry, ostensibly waiting for Owen and reinforcements from the farm. They could just as easily have met Owen elsewhere though, and not allow themselves to be cornered within the Armory.

Why did Brown change his plan?

I slapped my forehead when I realized what might be going on.

Our talks. Brown was impatient and must have decided that being a martyr would be the best way to further the cause of freedom for Blacks. He wanted freedom now, and not spread out over forty years.

And Dangerfield, father of seven, beloved husband, and my friend, was an acceptable casualty in Brown's view to achieve his objective.

♣ ♣ ♣

I was trapped in the watch house with several slaves and with Armory workers who were kidnapped when they reported to work that morning. None of Brown's men were guarding us, though, and would likely not return from the engine house because of the increased gunfire around us. For that same reason, none of us tried to escape.

The so-called troops mustered in formation near the hotel. They looked to be regular citizens working as a unit, possibly a local militia. I could only hear hammering from the engine house. No one was shooting as the troops eased ever closer to the Armory gate.

Suddenly, a salvo erupted from next door and Brown's men felled several troops, causing them to beat a hasty retreat. Men continued to fire upon our position, but they didn't risk exposing themselves again.

After a bit, the shooting stopped almost completely, but then gradually resumed. This time, however, most of the new gunfire was clearly not aimed at us, but farther up a side street where John Copeland and John Henry Kagi were stationed at the Rifle Works.

Although I couldn't see what was happening, the raucous shouts of the citizenry made it clear that things were not going well for Copeland and Kagi.

Brown obviously came to the same conclusion. Less than fifteen minutes later, he sent out William Thompson and a prisoner with a white flag of truce. Ignoring the flag, a rush of townspeople surrounded Thompson and took him away.

Clearly the rules of engagement were not in effect. As the defenders of the town of Harper's Ferry appeared to be devolving into a mob, I feared for all of our lives, raiders and hostages alike.

Evidently, Brown did not see things the same way I did, because a very short while later, Aaron Stevens, Watson Brown, and another hostage headed into the street with a white cloth tied to a pike. They made it as far as the Armory gate before shooting recommenced.

Watson was hit first, and then Stevens fell hard from multiple wounds. The hostage took the opportunity to flee and no one from the engine house fired upon him.

Watson, bleeding from the gut, began pulling himself along the street back towards the engine house while Stevens lay dying at the gate. My heart felt like it would burst from my chest. I could only watch impotently while both men suffered.

The scene played out in slow motion, as Watson managed to pick himself up enough to crawl while Stevens could only writhe in pain. Both sides of the conflict looked on with no one taking further action until Watson was nearly back at the engine house doorway.

Finally, Oliver Brown slid outside and hurriedly pulled his older brother back inside.

Now Stevens lay alone at the other end of the bloody trail made by poor Watson. I desperately wanted to do something, but despite spending nearly seven years as a police officer, I was afraid. I harbored no illusions about the mob in their current mood not gunning down a young Black man, and I was not yet ready to die again.

Incredibly, a lone hostage exited the engine house and walked bravely to Stevens' now inert form. I held my breath, fearing an overeager townsperson or militiaman might shoot, but no one did.

That solid, remarkably brave hero scooped Stevens up and carried him toward the hotel and, hopefully, medical treatment. I cried for the second time that day.

Inexplicably, about fifteen minutes later, the same intrepid hostage returned to the engine house and captivity. Not everyone in Harper's Ferry was without honor.

⚬ ⚬ ⚬

The quiet was soon broken when I heard gunshots from the direction of the Potomac River. Speculation was fruitless but I couldn't help but wonder. It could be any of the raiders not stationed at the engine house, or even Owen and his crew trying to reach Brown but meeting with resistance.

Every time I thought the situation could not be more disastrous, I was proven wrong. I had screwed with history by talking to Brown. Now the casualties were mounting.

Through the broken window, I could hear shouting from not too far away. I peered out and, because of the acute angle, I could barely see Dangerfield's body surrounded by some of the town's less refined citizens. Fortunately, it was doubtful anyone from within the engine house could see it at all.

A group of obviously inebriated, low-life scumbags were kicking the body and screaming unintelligibly at it. Man's inhumanity to man was on exhibit once again.

Aware that no one was firing at them from the engine house, two scavengers began tugging at Dangerfield's boots. Others poked at him with sticks. Then, when one of the subhuman creatures aimed a rifle at him, I shuddered and quickly looked away. At the crack of the rifle I jumped, and finally realized Brown may have been right in the first place.

Slavery would only end with bloodshed.

22

Playing Doctor

As I stared at the brass bucket in the corner, I thought to myself, I'm so glad to be a man.

I still waxed nostalgic about my breasts on occasion, but as a guy, it was nice not to worry about bras, shaving my underarms and legs, or worse, the monthly visits from Auntie Flo. And in my current situation, I was blissfully relieved to be the proud owner of a penis.

In the midst of the chaos, normal bodily functions proceeded, well, normally. If I were still my 41-year-old female self, the coffee I'd ingested would have run through me in thirty minutes or less, and the food would have followed soon after.

As a teenaged male, I'd lasted many hours before I finally gave in and urinated into the bucket in the corner like everyone else. Not a pretty sight, but far less awkward than if I were still physiologically female. Small favors. But I was not looking forward to the time when we needed the bucket for more than urine.

After seeing Dangerfield defiled, among other things, I decided I didn't want or need to further witness history unfold. I'd seen enough tragedy for a lifetime.

I needed to make sure that when the chance to escape presented itself, I was prepared. Circumstances dictated that I wait until dark, when the activity level outside would likely drop, before making my move. I migrated back to a cozy spot near the stove and tried to sleep, perchance to dream.

Surprisingly, sleep did come, albeit in brief increments. Not so surprisingly, the fitful sleep brought with it nightmares incorporating the sounds of gunfire and projectiles striking the building.

℘ ℘ ℘

The sound of glass shattering roused me for good.

I opened my eyes to see a group of armed men outside the rearmost side windows using rifle butts to clear glass from the window frames.

"Are any of the attackers in here?" someone shouted to us, assuming, I suppose, that any self-respecting raider would promptly identify himself as such. In truth, if any of Brown's men had been among us, they would have responded with a carefully aimed bullet or two.

To my relief, multiple men responded loudly, "No!"

"Is Colonel Washington here?" another voice asked.

"No suh," replied one of the slaves. "They took him and Massuh Allstadt over to the engine house."

"Damn! Let's at least get these men to safety for now."

Quickly, the rescuers began helping the hostages through the glass and away from the watch house area.

I held back, not wanting to be among the first out. My preference was to blend in with the rest of the Black men and slip away when possible.

The raiders in the engine house could not see what was going on, but shots were nonetheless being fired from the front doors and windows to keep the militia from storming Brown's fort. Militiamen fired back to occupy Brown and company during the rescue, making the entire scene a noisy, close-quarters battle.

As I was climbing out, one of rescuers who was laying down cover fire, a tall, slender teen, spun around and fell, wounded by a bullet to the upper chest area.

I stopped in my tracks when I heard the thwack of bullet entering flesh, partly in fear of being shot, but also from shock. Not for the first time did I sort of wish I were back on Bates' plantation harvesting tobacco.

Then the boy rolled over and made eye contact with both me and the man who was helping me through the jagged glass around the window frame.

Without a word, my rescuer and I looked at each other, nodded, and eased toward the bleeding lad. He lay just beyond the corner of the building, with his head closer to us. An acrid cloud of smoke from the discharge of weaponry hovered about chest high. The small-scale explosions from the Sharps and other rifles mere feet away were deafening, but slowing in frequency.

By mutual assent, we paused a few feet away from the boy, gathering our courage and watching for signs of danger. When it was apparent no rounds were heading our way from the engine house, we dashed out and each grabbed a shoulder, pulling the now unconscious boy to safety. Then we lifted him, each supporting a leg and shoulder, and carried him, following behind the other hostages and militiamen.

Our retreat followed the wall surrounding the Armory toward the gate. Once at the gate, more shooters laid down cover fire while we scurried through the opening.

A dark-haired, mustachioed man wearing a jacket with epaulets and a sword at his hip, pointed those of us helping the wounded toward the Wager House Hotel, the place that had supplied my most recent meal. As we approached the entrance, I looked out at Maryland Heights, the Potomac River, and the covered bridge I'd crossed the night before. Dark clouds still threatened to resume pelting the area with an icy rain, and I wasn't looking forward to trying to escape under those conditions.

"Thank you," moaned the young man in our arms, speaking for the first time since we scooped him up. He opened his eyes, leaned his head back, and looked steadily at each of us before again shutting his eyes and resting his chin on his chest.

Once inside the hotel, we were directed to take our wounded burden upstairs to what I assumed would be a triage area. While we shuffle-walked across the lobby, I looked around at the surprisingly upscale interior. To our left was a crowded bar made of beautiful polished wood, with enormous mirrors behind and candles illuminating it all. To our right, a massive fireplace warmed the busy dining area.

The warmth extended to the staircase, which we ascended carefully despite our growing weariness. Just beyond the top of the stairs, we passed an open room full of men surrounding a bed. Brown's right hand man, Aaron Stevens, occupied that bed.

We stopped outside the doorway and looked inside, unsure of where to go next. An older gentleman and a middle-aged woman stood over Stevens, both spattered with Stevens' blood. The woman looked up and said absently, "Across the hall. Clean his wound if you can. Someone will be over as soon as possible."

My fellow transporter replied, "Yes ma'am," and I nodded.

We carefully laid the young man on a bed and I began unbuttoning his jacket. My partner took a step back and watched with wide eyes.

"I better get back with my, uh, company," he stammered nervously. "Appreciate your help. He's a good kid."

It was clear that he wanted no part in providing first aid.

"What's his name?"

"Amos. Amos Johnson. I, uh, better go."

And with that, he backed out of the room, leaving me alone with the unconscious Amos.

The wound was in the right pectoral area. I removed the left jacket sleeve first, and then carefully slid off the right sleeve. Then I tried to do the same with his shirt, but the fabric was merged with the wound.

A jug of water, a basin, and a stack of washcloths and towels were on the bureau, so I used a moistened washcloth to loosen the dried blood and extract the fabric. The debridement and cleaning revealed a nasty wound that bled far less than I would have imagined.

Something didn't seem right. Considering all that I had done to him, Amos was remarkably quiet. And still.

His chest wasn't rising and falling. I leaned over his nose and listened. He wasn't breathing. All I could hear was the slight hiss of air escaping from his wound. I palpated his wrist, and no pulse either.

"Help," I yelled. "I need help. Patient not breathing!"

"Wake up, Amos," I commanded, shaking him futilely.

He remained still, so I dredged up my memories of CPR training from the police academy and the refresher courses. Chest compressions or breaths first? How many of each?

First, I figured I should cover the wound. A moist washcloth was all I had, so I used it.

Then I tilted his head back by lifting his neck from below. Finally, I pinched his nose, opened his mouth, and began exhaling into him hard enough to make his chest rise. Three is usually a good number, so I did three full breaths and yelled for help again.

Chest compressions. Interlaced fingers, palm of bottom hand pushes down on the center of the chest. Maybe fifteen or twenty compressions or so and then back to breathing, I guessed.

About ten compressions in, a smallish man wearing a brown, rumpled, wide brimmed farmers hat strolled into the room. He was clearly not a doctor, with a long rifle and powder horn draped over his shoulders.

"What the hell you doing to that boy, nigger!" he shouted before rushing to me and attempting to shove me away from Amos.

I say attempting because I stood firm, continuing the CPR. The plantation workout program had shaped me into a solid fellow, certainly able to withstand a half-hearted attempt by a smaller man expecting obeisance. Then I gave him a glare that warned him not to do it again. I had no idea what a glare from Matthew would look like, but apparently it got the message across.

I completed my compressions and went back to breaths. Bubbles were forming on the surface of the washcloth after I blew so I knew the wound wasn't sealed. I scanned the room while doing the next round of chest compressions, looking for something to form a seal around the hole in the lad's chest. I'd seen situations similar to this in the hospital E.R. back when I was a cop, and on TV more recently. The best I could do was to piece together what bits of knowledge I had and hope for the best.

"Candles. Get the candles," I ordered my ineffective assailant. He hesitated, so I almost gave him another glare, but opted instead to go with, "Please."

He hustled back with a burning candle in each hand.

"Pour the wax onto the washcloth."

He looked at me as if I were insane.

"He's got a sucking chest wound," I told my reluctant aide. "If we don't seal it soon, I think his lung will collapse."

"You ain't no doctor. How you know what gonna happen?"

"I don't. But he's not breathing and his heart has stopped, so it can't hurt. Maybe we can save him. I'm told he's a good kid."

My aide looked out toward the hallway, called for help, and then said, "Aw, what the hell." He poured the wax onto the washcloth, shaking his head the whole time. Then he returned the lit candles to their holders and grabbed two more.

Just as I was giving Amos a final breath before returning to chest compressions, the doctor that I had seen at Aaron Stevens' bedside entered the room.

"What the hell!?" exclaimed the doc, as my 'nurse' was dribbling the last bit of wax around the wounded area.

"Cardiopulmonary resuscitation, doctor. He wasn't breathing and his heart had stopped. Gunshot wound to right pectoral area. Air escaping through wound. We're trying to seal the wound to prevent a collapsed lung."

I lost count of the compressions as I spilled the information to the doc. I made a best guess and then went back to breathing.

The doctor took a quick pulse, and then used an odd stethoscope that had two chestpieces to listen to the heart.

"Weak pulse. Heart seems to be coming back on track. Whatever the hell you're doing, keep doing it until I get back with my nurse and my bag."

He dashed out and was back in seconds, accompanied by his nurse.

"As soon as he is stable, we must remove the bullet and any other foreign objects, and then suture the wound. Clean and lay out the forceps, extractors, probes and needles, Mrs. Stansbury."

The doctor listened to the heart again, and then looked across Amos at me.

"Heartbeat is reasonably regular and strong again. I assume you are somehow massaging the heart muscle by pressing down on his chest. It worked, so focus on providing breathing assistance. I've got to determine where the ball is."

He rolled Amos over slightly onto his left side and felt around along the boy's back. Then, after he'd laid the boy back down, the doctor sighed and rubbed his own forehead and temple.

"No exit wound, and I could not detect any indication the ball is near the surface of the back. I shall have to enter through the chest wound."

Mrs. Stansbury had laid out various primitive looking surgical instruments on a clean cloth atop a shiny metal tray. Then she began cutting off and carefully pulling away the remainder of Amos' clothing from his upper body. As she did, the doctor continued feeling along the torso, I suppose making sure the bullet had not ricocheted to a different area completely. All the while, I continued to breathe for Amos, watching his chest expand and relax.

Suddenly, Amos shuddered. I backed off and looked to the doctor for guidance.

"Just a moment," he said, leaning in close to Amos' head and listening.

He looked up, nodding and smiling. "He's back with us, breathing on his own."

I glanced over at the fellow who had shoved me earlier. His eyes were wide and he was shaking a bit, but he inclined his head and tipped his hat at me. That was probably as close as I would get to an apology, so I nodded back.

Mrs. Stansbury and the doctor continued their choreographed dance, cleaning and probing Amos in search of the hidden projectile.

"Good work, gentlemen," the doctor told us. Then, looking directly at me he said, "Stay close. I'd like to discuss that cardiopulmonary resuscitation procedure with you after we are done. What's your name, young man?"

"Matthew, sir."

"Ed, would you get Matthew a sandwich or something from downstairs, please. That's the least you can do for the young fellow who saved your nephew."

"Sure, doc," my erstwhile aide and new friend Ed replied.

"Well," I began, "Amos helped save me and quite a few others from the watch house. It's the least *I* could do."

Mrs. Stansbury cleared her throat loudly to remind the doctor they had more work to do, so I sat on the floor, relaxed my tense muscles, and let them get to it.

Surprisingly, I found that I enjoyed doing medical stuff. I'd seen plenty of blood and guts while with the police department, so I wasn't disturbed by it at all. As I waited for my sandwich, I made up my mind to consider looking into medicine as a new career here in the past.

I'd already started to nod off while waiting for Ed to return with my chow, so by the time my belly was full of roast beef, sleep came rapidly. When I awakened, no one was left in the candlelit room but me and the unconscious, but still living patient, Amos.

A bit groggy, I decided to pour some water into the basin and use one of the clean washcloths to wipe the sleep from my eyes and to freshen up in general. It felt a bit indulgent, but it perked me right up. A pedicure and massage would have been lovely too, but I reckoned I felt pretty enough for the time being.

I pulled on my coat and hat, took a deep breath to calm myself, and peered out into the hallway. From the bar downstairs, faint voices and the sounds of glasses clinking could be heard, but things were quiet up here.

I turned and crossed the room to look outside the window. Regular military had joined with the local militia in watching over Brown and the engine house. The presence of more troops was a negative for my departure plans.

However, it was full dark outside, the ideal time to escape and put distance between Harper's Ferry, Virginia and myself. Assuming all, or at least most eyes were on the engine house, I had a chance. I was mildly curious about how Amos would fare, but not curious enough to hang around another day. The situation in Harper's Ferry would surely get worse before it got better.

Now was the time to seek out an unguarded exit and keep to the shadows.

23

Shadows

My plan was simple – find an exit and use it. If anyone asked, I would say I was looking for the facilities.

I opened the door and looked both ways down the hallway. No one was in sight. The door to Aaron Stevens' room was shut, but I could hear faint voices from inside.

I turned left, away from the main stairwell, hoping for an emergency exit. The thought occurred to me that in my time, such an exit would be marked, "Emergency Exit Only – Door Alarm Will Sound." Of course, in my time, I could also use an elevator and not worry about being sold South. And my plan to claim to be in search of a rest room would be absurd since indoor plumbing in every suite was de rigueur.

Unfortunately, the Wager House Hotel was not up to code for the year 1999, lacking an emergency exit. I took a deep breath to calm myself and headed back to the central stairs, ready to act like one of my students asking for a hall pass to go to the restroom.

At the bottom of the stairs, a regular soldier in a blue uniform stood guard, along with a militiaman I recognized from the rescue at the watch house.

On my approach, the soldier stepped in front of me and said, "State your business."

Remembering how I responded when one of my students gave a long, drawn out excuse, I decided to just answer, "Outhouse."

The militiaman smiled at the soldier, saying, "This here boy helped carry one of our fellers up to the doc."

Then he turned to me and pointed, saying, "Just go out the door and round that way to the back for the Negro outhouse. Watch out for stray bullets, boy. Some of the fellers is getting pretty liquored up."

The soldier motioned to the door with his head and I walked outside, pleased to see part one of my plan go so smoothly.

$\wp \wp \wp$

As I headed toward the outhouse, I realized I actually needed to take advantage of the facilities. Two likely wooden structures were in the rear of the hotel. The larger, more respectable looking building had two doors, one of which had a crescent moon shaped hole cut into the door. The second was a bit apart and more ramshackle. Once I got closer in the dark, I could read the signs above the doors – Men, Women, Negro. Of course, I didn't need to be able to read to know which outhouse to use.

My brother Eliot always joked about how he figured ladies rooms were posh, well-appointed and even clean, while men's rooms were none of the above. I found myself curious as to how the outhouses compared to one another, but decided it would be safer and more expedient to simply do my business and hightail it as far from Harper's Ferry as I could.

Once inside the Negro outhouse, I felt like I'd hit the jackpot. Sure, it was just a hole in the ground, but firstly, it didn't smell half as bad as I'd anticipated. I've been in smellier 20th century portapotties. Most importantly, however, was that in addition to the bucket of corncobs made available for wiping oneself, someone had left a newspaper. Maybe this would be my lucky night.

♪ ♪ ♪

Or not.

Immediately after I exited the powder room, I rounded a corner and froze. I found myself face-to-face with an unfamiliar, musket-wielding militiaman. Sporting a dark beard and a long, black duster, he reacted to my presence by pressing his gun's muzzle into my gut. At first glance, very intimidating.

"Where, where do you think you are, are goin', nigger ... nigger?" he slurred at me, immediately lowering the intimidation factor.

"Home, suh," I answered, trying to sound as deferential as I could.

"How, how do I know you, you ain't one of them raiders?" he barked, weaving a bit at the effort of speaking and training a weapon on me at the same time.

"Well suh, I ain't got no gun or nothing."

Silence. He struggled to process my statement, and just when it appeared his mental circuits might overload, he came to a conclusion.

"Maybe, maybe I should take you to the law, nigger."

I assessed the odds of disarming him without him firing a shot, which would either harm me or alert others to my location. Iffy. I decided to try to get his finger out of the trigger guard before doing anything stupid. And something stupid was definitely under consideration.

"Just point me which way you wants me to go, suh, and I'll go there," I said, looking in all directions as if lost.

"Stupid nigger," he grumbled, "just go round that way." He shifted the rifle to his left arm so that he could point with his right hand.

Gotta love a pliable drunk.

I nodded vigorously, but instead of moving away, I stepped in and jerked the gun out of his hand. At the same time, I kicked him in the testicles, kneed him in the gut and swung a vicious backfist to his right temple area.

He fell to the ground silently, my efficiency indubitably aided by his blood alcohol level.

I dragged him to a grassy area and positioned him as if he were sleeping off his liquor. Then I hid his gun in the bushes and removed his knife from his waist, hiding it under my jacket.

I turned to walk away, but realized my crapulous militiaman might have more to offer. Upon checking his pockets, I found money, which could come in handy. Then I realized he was about my size, and his clothing looked far warmer and newer than my own.

In for an inch, in for a klick.

It just made sense to take a little extra time to supplement my wardrobe with his high-collared shirt, warm woolen trousers, spiffy vest, full-length duster, boots, and gloves. And to show there were no hard feelings, I even took the time to put my trousers on him up to his knees, and slip my gently used shoes on his feet to protect him from the cool, evening air. Then I blanketed his upper body with my well-worn shirt and coat.

I considered taking his musket too, but decided I'd be better off without it. In the current climate, a Black man with a weapon might be fired upon without discussion. Besides, the militiaman's weapon only had one shot, and I wasn't completely sure how it worked. Instead, I disabled it by grinding the barrel into the ground to bung it up with the soft soil from the intermittent rain.

One obstacle down.

Quick assessment. I now had warm, dark clothing and money. No one was looking for me specifically. Home was less than 200 miles away.

All I needed was a getaway car.

As a cop, I'd observed that the guilty party is usually the party who acts guilty. As long as I acted like I belonged and didn't panic, I'd merely be one of many Black people going about his business. But just to be on the safe side, I'd try to avoid being seen at all.

♂ ♂ ♂

I made my way to the end of the alley. The bridge across the Potomac was just a few dozen yards away. The train station was right there too, and I fantasized about using the benevolent militiaman's funds to buy a ticket and board like any anonymous passenger. Unfortunately, my skin color made me unable to blend in, and the military presence at the station and bridge would surely stop me from boarding the train or even just walking across the footbridge to Maryland.

That's when it hit me that I could hop a train like a hobo to make my way north.

The more I thought about it, the more I realized it was a decent plan. Clearly, I couldn't hop the train on this side of the river because of all of the soldiers, but once across the river, I could easily do it. I'd seen it done in movies and on TV, and I was a young, healthy, vigorous lad. Should be a piece of cake once I figured out how to cross the river. The quite wide and powerful river.

I turned left from the alley, staying in the shadows, until I saw an opportunity to work my way to the riverbank. Three drunken militiamen fired their guns into the air near the bridge, capturing the attention of the soldiers. I casually made my way to the thicket at the water's edge and disappeared from sight.

Looking out across the Potomac, I could see a huge rock not far from shore and a large river island beyond that. If I bundled up my clothes and boots, I could probably make it that far unscathed, if a bit damp.

After that, however, the current would carry me upriver, possibly into hidden rocks that could knock me out and lead to an ugly death by drowning.

I decided to pick my way along the shore and look for better options. The night was still youngish and I hadn't heard a train whistle.

Twenty or thirty minutes later, I hadn't found anything better and had already passed the junction of the Potomac and the Shenandoah River. I sat on a convenient rock and considered whether to turn back. Things were quieter here, although I could still hear the occasional report of gunfire.

I could also hear a low moan somewhere to my right, out in the water.

I eased in that direction and, once I focused, I could plainly see a man lying spread-eagle on a rock about fifteen feet from shore. I was curious, but also cautious. My priority was escaping intact. If the man on the rock were another drunkard, he'd be fine where he was until daybreak.

At least that's what I told myself.

Something about his moans, the gurgling quality, convinced me to take a quick look. I took off my duster and my boots, rolled up my trouser legs, and waded to him.

I recognized his face immediately. It was Lewis Leary, one of the Black raiders. He'd arrived less than two days ago and we were on the Col. Washington mission together mere hours ago.

Up close, he was a mess. Blood everywhere. It was clear he'd suffered multiple gunshot wounds and substantial blood loss. His skin was ashen and cold to the touch.

He looked up at me and asked in a shaky voice, "Is that you, Matthew?"

"Yes, it's me, Mr. Leary."

I recalled that he'd told me he was married and had a baby back in Ohio where he'd worked as a harness maker. He was a handsome man, and earnest about the cause. Now he was undoubtedly dying.

"How it look?"

I wasn't sure what he was referring to, but, truth be told, nothing looked good.

"Not good, sir. Mr. Newby is dead, and Watson and Stevens are both shot up pretty bad."

"I don't like all this water round me. Can you get me up out of here?"

"Sure. Sure I can."

And I did, positioning him in thick, dry grass uphill a bit from the water.

"Anything else?" I asked.

"If, if you ever happen to make it to Oberlin, tell my family." He paused and closed his eyes for a minute. When his eyes fluttered opened again, he continued through clenched teeth, "Tell them I died doing the right thing. The right thing for our people."

"I will. Try to rest now, okay?"

I turned away, unsure of what to do next. Finally, I pulled my boots and duster back on and rolled down my trouser legs. When I turned back to check on Leary, he surprised me with what he said next.

"I'm ready to die now," he announced, trembling.

"What?"

"I know I'm hurt real bad. All over. I'm ready to die now. Will you do it?"

I understood what he was asking and why. I was not unsympathetic. Even with the best 20th century medical treatment, he would probably die. With 19th century medicine, death was a given; yet I was hesitant.

Before every shift that I worked as a police officer, I reminded myself that I might have to kill someone in order to protect myself or someone else. At the time, I felt prepared to do it if necessary. But to kill someone I knew, if only slightly, was a wholly different situation. Despite knowing death would be a mercy for Leary, it didn't feel right to take a life so soon after saving one. Could I just kill a man?

"Please," he croaked, before closing his eyes again. He was clearly in tremendous pain.

Finally, I had to put myself in his place. He might hang on for hours, on the edge of death. Worse yet, a mob like those who abused Dangerfield might discover him and savagely torture poor Leary to death.

"Yes," I reluctantly agreed, with no idea as to how to go about it.

I still had the militiaman's knife, so I could cut the carotid. He'd already lost so much blood that he would probably bleed out in seconds. Too painful for both of us I decided.

I could drown him, but he'd already told me he didn't like the water. Or I could suffocate him. That would be tidy and somehow not as grisly.

"Are you sure?" I asked.

He lay there in the grass, eyes shut, chest heaving. "Yes."

"Okay. Okay. I think the best way is to cover your nose and mouth until you can no longer breathe. Is that acceptable?"

He nodded weakly.

Like with any unpleasant task, the best thing to do is to just do it. I pinched his nostrils closed with my left hand and covered his mouth with my right. My intention was to watch his chest, and when it no longer rose and fell, to hold on for thirty seconds more.

I couldn't look, though. Instead, I thought of anything except what I was doing. He was so feeble that he didn't even struggle reflexively.

After what seemed like a sufficient amount of time, I lifted my hands. A glance showed he was not moving. He seemed at peace.

I'd have plenty of time to process the morality of what I'd done later.

What I had to do now was to skedaddle, and figure out how the heck I was going to cross two large rivers in the dead of night without getting caught, shot or drowned.

24

From the Muddy Banks of the Potomac

As luck would have it, less than five minutes later I stubbed a toe as I literally stumbled upon a simple rectangular flat-bottomed boat with a long handled rudder in back. It was about eight feet by ten feet, and tied off to a tree near the water.

I'd never managed a craft like this before, but since the Shenandoah was flowing to the Potomac, I figured all I had to do was steer.

I untied the boat and carried the rope onboard with me. As I'd thought, the current jerked the boat from the shore, nearly knocking me over. I played with the rudder and quickly figured out the basics of how to steer.

In no time at all, I was in the choppier waters of the Potomac and straining to maintain control. The rudder

235

bent but didn't break as I forced the flatboat toward the northern shore of the Potomac.

For a moment, I entertained the idea of floating even farther downriver, away from the chaos of Harper's Ferry. Then I heard the whistle of a train and decided I could always return to the boat if I missed the train.

I tried to ease my way to the shore, but the water inexplicably began moving faster, and the boat struck rock after rock. Up ahead, the water sounded even rougher.

My knowledge of the geography of this part of the country sucked. Could there be a waterfall ahead? Whitewater rapids? My mind wanted to panic, but I knew that wouldn't accomplish a darned thing.

I just continued making incremental progress toward the north shore until finally, the boat's hull scraped on the rocky riverbank. I jumped out with the rope, pulled the boat a bit more aground, and tied it to a nearby sapling. Hopefully the owner would spot it in the daylight.

The inland vegetation was dense, but I knew the train followed the course of the river for some distance. I just needed to locate the track.

By this time, I could actually hear the train itself, the brakes squealing as it stopped by the Wager House Hotel.

The bank angled sharply upwards, plus it was wet from all the rain, so I took an extra minute to find an easier route up. I maneuvered my way along the

236

slippery rocks until I found a place where I could get a handhold on some tree roots that extended down from the top of the bank.

A few steps out of the thicket was a pathway, and a hundred feet beyond that, a rise that had to contain the railroad track. I crossed the path and stopped. Just in front of me, the moon was reflecting off something wide and shiny. Water!

A canal. Who digs a canal between a river and a railroad track? Talk about redundancy.

Canals are usually less than ten feet deep, and sometimes as shallow as five or six feet. I knew this from teaching history and geography. Since this canal was only fifty feet or so across, it would be an easy but time-consuming swim. Nonetheless, I didn't want to get any wetter than I had to considering the weather.

What else did I know about canals? They usually have locks to adjust the water level. I could get lucky and find a lock or bridge across. If not, I'd have to quickly strip down and float across.

I turned to the right on the pathway, away from Harper's Ferry and the train, and began to jog.

I knew that the farther I got from the station, the faster the train would be moving when I tried to hop it. However, I also recalled that the bridge from Harper's Ferry had a sharp curve on either side, and the train wouldn't be able to really begin accelerating until a good bit after it crossed the Potomac. Running in this direction would buy me a few extra seconds of time and add extra distance between me and the armed forces securing the town.

After a hundred or so yards, I began to wonder if there had been a lock just left of where I'd started, and I'd run in the wrong direction. In my haste, I'd barely glanced that way.

After another hundred yards or so, I considered turning back. The all-aboard whistle of the train convinced me otherwise. I ran faster.

Less than fifty yards later, I was rewarded with the sight of a wooden structure crossing the canal. To get across the canal, I would have to maneuver along the top edges of a lock gate, not much wider than a balance beam. It would be tricky in full daylight and I expected it would be far more difficult in the moonlight.

As I began cautiously putting one foot in front of the other along the rickety gate, I heard two long whistles from the train. I figured that had to mean it was moving forward, so I did the same with renewed urgency. The gate rattled and shook under my weight, but I maintained my balance until just before I made it across.

My left foot twisted downward over the edge of the lock and I fell to my knees, teetering on the brink of falling in. I was so nervous I decided to straddle the gate and slid forward the remaining distance before trying to stand again.

Just as I was across, I could hear the clatter of the train on the track and feel the earth moving.

A small house with its lights off was to my right, and directly ahead was the rise leading to the tracks. I scrambled up the muddy slope, only slipping once, and stepped across the tracks. The train was so close that its vibrations rattled my teeth.

I wasn't the only one who heard and felt the train. A lantern now lit the small house and a door opened. A man stepped out and looked toward the tracks, but he didn't seem to see me. Wearing the long, black duster of the militiaman in combination with my dark skin, I was practically invisible as I leaned against the wall of the cliff that the railroad track paralleled.

Thanks to Matthew's strong, young body, I easily recovered from my exertions and began to focus on my next task. In the movies, it looked pretty straightforward. Run alongside the massive iron beast, grab the ladder or hop in the open boxcar, and, most importantly, avoid getting squished.

I had a decent straightaway to run along, so my expectation was that it would be pretty simple. What I hadn't considered was the fact that the train was an 1859 model and not a 1999 model.

And it was a passenger train.

The noise was deafening as the engine passed first, picking up speed now that it was past the curves. The cars were lit, and I could see passengers and conductors and such, both seated and milling about.

What I couldn't see were ladders attached to the sides, or boxcars with open doors inviting me to clamber aboard. Car after car went by, and I realized I had to make a move before the train was moving too fast or the caboose appeared.

Once I realized neither ladders nor inviting boxcars would manifest, I noticed that each car had steps at both the back and front, lower to the ground than either a ladder or boxcar. The rearmost cars looked to be empty or nearly empty, so I timed the interval and ran alongside, hopping aboard as if it were an extremely noisy and fast-moving San Francisco cable car.

☙ ☙ ☙

Because the interior of the cars was illuminated and it was dark outside, I felt secure in my invisibility. I hooked an arm around the handrail and sat uncomfortably on the hard, metal platform outside the door to the car. My recently acquired duster was a godsend, despite my somewhat less than godly method of acquisition. When I turned up the collar and buttoned it fully, it kept the worst of the wind from ripping through me.

With naught else to do, I began planning my next move. I didn't know exactly where the train was going other than eastward, away from Harper's Ferry.

I'd seen the letters B&O on the side of the cars, which told me I was on the Baltimore and Ohio line. If the train route terminated in Baltimore, I'd still have a ways to go to get to Philly. Most significantly, I'd still be in Maryland, a slave state, and thus my freedom could easily become forfeit again.

Just as my brain was realizing that a passenger train might have frequent stops that I would have to work around, the train whistle blew and it began slowing. I stuck my head around my side of the car and couldn't see anything resembling civilization. Then I carefully crawled across the platform to look at the other side, and saw a small, mostly dark station ahead.

To avoid detection, I knew I'd have to jump off once the train had slowed sufficiently. Instead of slowing more, however, it began to pick up speed again. My best guess was that I was lucky enough to have hopped an express train that only stopped when there were passengers to drop off or pick up.

The train repeated the slow and go cycle six more times before finally stopping in a town called Frederick. It was clear it would stop when I spotted a bright lantern hanging from a pole by the depot.

Unfortunately, this depot was in the center of a moderately large town with no woods or obvious places of concealment for me. I jumped off a good hundred yards before the train fully stopped and walked briskly but nonchalantly along the deserted street.

By the time the train had unloaded and loaded, I had hustled past the depot to a less well-lit area that I deemed safe for my reboarding, as it were.

Once I was safely back on my perch, I congratulated myself on my success at escaping Harper's Ferry. I also realized Brown had kept his promise to me. By leaving me amongst the hostages, I was less likely to be a target for marksmen and more likely to have an opportunity to slip away unnoticed.

The train's next stop was in Mt. Airy, according to the sign at the depot. A single passenger, female, boarded. The stop was so brief that I had to break into a full run when the whistle sounded, as I hadn't yet gotten into position to discreetly reboard. It was still full dark and, other than in the train depot, Mt. Airy was as sleepy a hamlet as one could hope for in October of 1859.

Once I was back on my perch, I thanked whatever gods may be for Matthew's fast-twitch muscles. I thought I'd gotten back unnoticed, but that was not the case.

I heard a tap on the glass above me from inside the car. The young woman who had boarded the train in Mt. Airy was straining to see me in the dark.

I could see her quite clearly though. She was lovely.

Tall, but not excessively so. Wavy copper-colored hair pulled tight beneath a wide-brimmed cloth bonnet that matched her light blue dress, just visible under her red woolen jacket. Her skin was smooth and unblemished, appearing slightly tanned. Her brow was crinkled and her full lips were pulled back in a quizzical expression.

I was relieved to see she wasn't trying to attract the attention of the conductor or other train personnel. I put a finger to my lips and tried to look like I was pleading for her silence, which I suppose I was.

It seemed to work as she nodded and left the window without further ado.

Because there was so much else to worry about, I decided not to worry about her ratting me out and to instead focus on a strategy for what to do once I arrived in Baltimore.

I knew from talks with William Still that Baltimore had a substantial population of free Blacks. Ideally, I could blend in with them since it was a large urban area where strangers would be less likely to stand out.

The sun was beginning to rise, which meant I would soon no longer be an invisible man.

The train only made one other stop before reaching the Baltimore terminal. The setting was bucolic, providing me with plenty of cover for disembarking and re-embarking.

When I was back on board, so to speak, I again heard a tap on the glass above me. The young woman graced me with a tenuous half-smile and another slight nod before returning to her seat.

What was going on in her mind, I wondered?

While I wondered, I began running my fingers through my hair, trying to make myself more presentable.

25

Sweet Caroline

Baltimore was nothing like any of the prior stations. Were it not for the early hour, I would have surely been pointed out to the train personnel by concerned citizens as the train lumbered through the expansive city.

I had no idea where to get off and realized I was truly at a loss as to what to do next. While I was in a much better position than I occupied in Harper's Ferry, I still had a ways to go before I was home free.

Baltimore smelled and felt a lot like Philadelphia to me, although it took a couple of minutes to figure out why. The ocean! Salt water in the distance, and steam from the engine and horse manure nearby combined to trigger memories of my adopted home. It had the same feel as the Delaware River and the docks.

For the third time, I heard a tap on the glass above me. I looked up to see the same winsome young woman making sure she caught my eye. With hand signals, she motioned for me to stay down and to wait for her when the train stopped. Lacking a better plan, I nodded my compliance.

As the train pulled into the Camden Street Station, I stayed put. I glanced up again and saw the woman standing by the door that opened to my perch.

"Stay close to me and act as if I were your mistress," she whispered urgently as she exited the car. "Take my bag and follow behind me."

Again, lacking any better plan, I complied.

My new friend led me out of the busy station to the intersection of Howard Street and Camden Street where we boarded a horse-drawn streetcar. I'd seen such cars in Philadelphia but never ridden in one. This one looked almost brand new, or at least freshly painted in red, green, and gold.

She led me to the rear of the car and instructed me to sit in the very back row while she sat on the bench one row forward of mine. We were alone for a moment while the other passengers boarded, so I said a quick thank you.

"You are quite welcome," she replied without turning to look at me. "No more talking until I say we may speak safely."

I leaned back and looked around. The city really did feel like Philadelphia to my 20th century eyes, ears, nose, and general sensibilities.

The streetcar pulled away smoothly on the rails along Howard Street for a couple of blocks and then turned right on Pratt Street. We continued on Pratt for some distance past numerous docks on the right and businesses on the left. I envisioned Matthew's father going to work about now, and wondered about Oleta and William Still and my friend George. Would I soon see them again?

The horses rounded the corner on President Street, continuing to the President Street train station. When the car stopped, we stayed seated a little longer while the other passengers disembarked.

"My name is Miss Caroline. What should I call you?"

"Matthew."

I recalled that William Still's ten-year-old daughter shared the same name. Actually, she would probably be eleven by now. Thinking about her got me to thinking about Boy and Oleta. While I was daydreaming, Miss Caroline continued to speak.

"Once we get off the streetcar, continue to follow behind me. I'm going to try to get us passage on the next train to Philadelphia. Once there, I can direct you to people who will assist you in getting somewhere safe."

"If it's all the same to you, Miss Caroline, I'll just stay in Philadelphia. I have family and friends there. Do you need money for tickets? I have a few coins if that will help."

When I finished speaking, Caroline did a double take and said, "Oh."

After a moment, she stood, smoothed her dress, and said, "All right. Let us go. No talking please."

The President Street station was immense and busy. It was a great place to hide in plain sight.

At a fruit stand outside the station, Caroline purchased apples for each of us. We sat on a bench, not so close together as to draw attention, and proceeded to eat and talk.

I gave her the Cliff's Notes version of my adventures, leaving out any mention of John Brown for fear that any association with him might cause her to reconsider helping me. Once I'd finished, I asked her *why* she was helping me.

"I assume the best of my fellow man until otherwise indicated. Slavery is a repellent institution, and if I can in any small way subvert it, I shall."

"I applaud your stance, Miss Caroline. And again, thank you."

She laughed.

"You do not have to call me that when we are alone, Matthew. You are as free as I, and based on your speech, as educated as I."

"Perhaps, although my friends never hesitate to point out my lack of Latin."

248

She smiled at that. I liked her smile, and liked that I triggered it.

We sat quietly for a couple of minutes, enjoying our fruit.

Finally, I broke the silence, asking, "Have you ever done this before?"

"No. The opportunity has never presented itself until today."

"Where are you headed?"

"Back to school in Philadelphia. I am currently studying literature, but I hope to someday enter the Female Medical College of Pennsylvania."

"Impressive. Funny you mention that, because I was very recently contemplating a career in medicine."

"I suspect you and I will both face obstacles, but what is life without challenges?"

"Helping me is a huge risk, and could ruin your dream if we're caught. So, again, thank you."

"Actually, I have another reason for helping you."

She got quiet, uncertain if she should go on. I decided not to press and waited for her to decide whether to continue.

"You see," she began, "I am a quadroon. My mother and brother are slaves. My father is their master."

"Wow," I gasped. "So how is it that you are free?"

"My mother convinced Father to send me away to boarding school when I was seven. I was raised in the big house and was always acknowledged as the master's daughter. I looked and sounded as White as anyone else, so he consented to sending me away, telling me to make him proud. I think I have. Yet I have never been formally freed."

"What about your mother and brother?"

"They are too dark to pass as White. Mother is nonetheless the acknowledged mistress of the house, and Benjamin works as a groom. For slaves, they live well, but living well is not the same as living free. Sometimes I wonder if Father is keeping them there just to ensure that I visit. In my more cynical moments, I suspect he has not freed me because he is still uncertain of my affections. And as I grow older, I do find myself more uncertain, so I suppose he is right in his way."

I did not know how to respond to that, so we had another stretch of silence between us.

"We should get our tickets now," Caroline said.

I followed her silently.

After getting tickets and a snack, we went back to the bench to wait. The next train wouldn't depart for over an hour.

Our conversation turned to a less personal topic, as we discussed Austen, Dickens, Cooper, Stowe, and other writers with whom we were both familiar. Caroline was surprised that I loved Austen, and I was surprised by her appreciation of Cooper.

250

The hour went by quickly and before we knew it, it was time to board the train and resume our act of being mistress and slave. Caroline played her role well, asking the conductor where her boy should sit.

I went to the back of the car without hesitation or looking up. I was one small indignity from freedom.

We must have been on the train for five or six hours by my reckoning. I alternated between enjoying the scenery and nodding off due to a relatively sleepless night of train hopping. Caroline appeared to be doing the same from what I could tell, as I could only see the back of her head.

When the train began slowing to pull into the Philadelphia station, I awakened for the last time on this crazy ride, pleased to see sights I hadn't seen for far too long. I could barely believe I had somehow fumbled and lucked my way back to freedom. It seemed like a lifetime ago I'd followed Harriet to Maryland and was captured.

I met Caroline just outside the train and walked into the station with her.

"I suppose at the very least I should see you home safely," I said.

"That would be nice," she replied with a shy smile.

"Should we walk or hail a cab?"

"Let's walk. It's not too far."

I continued carrying her bag as she led the way. I still maintained a bit of distance between us because, despite being in Philadelphia, the year was still 1859.

"So," I began, "do any of your friends or classmates know your, uh, whole story?"

"Oh, heavens no," Caroline responded in a quietly aghast tone. "Everyone knows that I am from the South and my father owns a plantation, but absolutely no one knows that he also owns my mother and brother. That would complicate my life in ways too numerous to consider. Assuming I were allowed to continue in school, I would be treated as a pariah."

"I guess it would complicate things," I said softly, understanding her situation and pushing the germ of an idea that we could be friends out of my mind.

"I want to believe that at some point soon, men will realize the folly of slavery. I want to believe that during my lifetime, I will be able to be myself, and walk freely with my entire family."

"I do too, but as long as it is profitable and legal, the South won't easily give it up. They'll need a nudge."

Caroline laughed.

"Oh yes. A nudge. You, sir, are a master of the understatement."

I wanted to tell her about Lincoln and gradual emancipation, but I didn't want her to think I was crazy. I was also beginning to seriously question what I assumed I knew about history.

252

Instead we talked about family and friends, and her studies.

Sooner than I wanted, she stopped and said, "I'm just ahead there in 708. I probably shouldn't be seen with you. Uncomfortable questions and all."

"I understand," I said, and I did.

If this were 1999, I would have mustered the courage to ask for her phone number. But in 1859, all I could do was return her bag and say goodbye. So I did, and turned to walk away.

"Wait, Matthew."

I turned to face her.

"Write, please. Caroline Vickers. 708. I'll write back. I promise."

Her facial expression and tone told me what she could not say or express in public in 1859. I smiled back, a warmth and relief spreading through my body.

"I will. Write, that is. Soon."

For some reason, I was tongue-tied. You'd think I'd never flirted with a woman while in the body of a young man.

Finally, after several seconds of awkward silence, I said, "Thank you for saving me, Miss Caroline."

Another smile.

Then she pivoted away from me, walking lightly on the balls of her feet and saying in a singsong voice, "You're quite welcome, Mr. Matthew."

26

Family Reunion

I knew that once I arrived home, neither Boy nor Matthew's family would let me leave for some time.

For that reason, I decided to first visit my erstwhile employer, William Still. I hoped he would have some ideas or advice to add to my nascent plan to return South to free Boy's family.

"*Salve, bone vir, a la carte!*" I said sheepishly as I entered Still's office.

Still's face erupted into a broad smile as he rushed to me and enveloped me in a bear hug. I immediately noticed that I was taller relative to Still than I had been. And broader in the shoulders.

"Your Latin has not improved in your absence," he chided, but I detected moisture in his eyes.

"Unfortunately, no," I grinned. "Sorry I forgot to notify you of my impromptu vacation. My circumstances changed rapidly."

"Harriet told me you disappeared while she was asleep. I imagine you have quite a tale to tell."

"That I do," I began, and I related the short version of my adventures over the last many months.

When I finished, Still leaned back in his chair and dropped his shoulders as if relieved of a burden.

"For your safety, I would never mention the John Brown connection again. Tensions are quite high as things unfold in Virginia. Nevertheless, you've had enough adventure for two lifetimes. Yet, I suspect it is not over."

It was my turn to sigh. After a moment, I explained to Still my rough plan for rescuing Mr. Thomas and Paula from the Bates Plantation.

He looked at me in silence, shook his head, and finally said, "Methinks we'll need our friend George's help with this."

⚯ ⚯ ⚯

Boy and Oleta essentially tackled me when I opened the door to the house. Momma half-fainted. Daddy caught my eye and nodded. Grandma slept on in her rocker.

The already overcrowded rooms were now bursting at the seams, but after what I'd been through, it felt great to be back in this out-of-time substitute for a home.

255

I gave them a heavily censored version of my adventures and left out any mention of returning South.

Later though, after everyone else was asleep, Boy rolled over on our pallet and asked when we were going back to get his father and sister.

I groggily whispered, "Soon."

♗ ♗ ♗

I slept in the next day, oblivious to the sounds of the adults getting ready and leaving for work. When I finally arose, only Boy was still at home.

"Where's Oleta?" I asked.

"School," Boy replied matter-of-factly.

I beamed. Something I would have to thank William Still for when I next saw him.

"What do you do all day while they're gone?" I asked.

"I clean and I read and I study Oleta's lessons. We make a copy of whatever she does for school and I do what I can. I read and spell better, but she is better at ciphering."

And the surprises just kept coming. I smiled with pride, knowing I had started something for them both. At the very least, planted a seed.

"Tell you what, Boy. I'll help you with your chores, but then I've got to go out for a bit."

"Can I go?"

"Not this time, but soon."

Boy and I tidied up, did the dishes, and emptied the chamber pots. Once I had him settled in to study, it was well after noon.

"I'll be back in an hour or two," I told Boy as I headed out.

♂ ♂ ♂

Freedom felt like a vacation. I wasn't constantly on the alert for slave catchers, overseers, or any ordinary citizen who decided to whack-a-Black out of frustration at his or her own plight.

The walk to George's office at the docks was pleasant and carefree, unlike my recent treks.

I rapped on his door and entered after he called out, "Entrez!"

George looked up from his paperwork and flashed a wide grin.

"Welcome back, my time-hopping friend. William told me of your return. We feared the worst after the story Harriet related. And then when the boy arrived and told us about your stay with John Brown, we could only assume your luck ran out at the Ferry."

"Still alive and kicking, George."

"And none the wiser, based on what William related to me this morning."

"I promised Boy's father I would be back."

"He doesn't actually expect you to return, Matthew! Uh, Eleanor."

"Either name is fine. But Mr. Thomas and Paula deserve to know what happened to Boy. And they deserve to be reunited with him. And to be free."

"I understand," he nodded. "I believe it to be patently stupid and exceedingly risky, but I understand. I promised William I would try to talk sense into you, so I have fulfilled my duty."

"Can you . . . will you help?" I asked softly.

"Of course. A gentleman will always help a lady, no matter how masculine her appearance," George quipped. "We have a fund established to finance activities such as the one on which you are about to foolishly embark."

I curtsied deeply, eliciting a chortle.

After I went over the list of supplies I'd need with George, we shook hands, hugged, and said our farewells. He said he could have everything ready in two days.

ℰ ℰ ℰ

Despite my certainty that I must return to the plantation, a reality wave washed over me as I exited George's office. If caught, I could be enslaved again, maimed, or worse yet, tortured and killed.

I glanced behind me toward the docks before turning onto the road into town and was surprised to see I'd acquired a shadow. Boy.

I waved him over to join me and we walked home together.

Since I wouldn't leave for more than another full day, I opted not to immediately tell Matthew's family or Boy that I was returning to the South.

ᵒ ᵒ ᵒ

The next 24 hours felt about as normal as one could imagine for a gal who was displaced in both time and body.

Oleta and Boy had each made significant strides forward with their educations.

Oleta, who had been an indifferent if not outright reluctant student before, was now eager and competitive, especially with Boy in mathematics. Boy read compulsively, be it books, product packaging, labels, or signs.

Whether I survived my rescue mission or not, they would be fine. The learning seed had taken root.

On the evening before my departure, I picked up the supplies I had requested from George. The two bundles were fairly heavy, but the months of labor on the plantation and natural physical development had altered my physique significantly enough that I could heft them without much difficulty.

George was businesslike in his interaction with me, explaining by rote how to use the items he'd gotten from the apothecary.

As I turned to exit though, he whispered just loud enough for me to hear, "Godspeed."

ᵒ ᵒ ᵒ

As soon as I entered the home of Matthew's family, which was now for all intents my family, Momma and the kids began peppering me with questions. I suppose I knew my bundles couldn't go unnoticed.

I sat them all down and explained the one final thing that I had to do.

"When do we go?" Boy asked.

"I have to go alone. It's too dangerous to have you come along. I'll be back in four or five days at the most."

"They my family. I can help," Boy insisted.

"Matthew right, Boy," Daddy spoke up, surprising us all. "He a man now, old enough to decide to do something dumb on his own. If you get hurt, yo daddy gone be ... he gone be hurt too, more than you can think."

That was by far the longest speech I'd ever heard from Daddy. Maybe Matthew's absence affected him more than I'd considered.

Boy looked at him, and then to Momma, who nodded in agreement with Daddy.

Finally, he looked at me, his brow furrowed. I think he was hoping for a change of heart from me, but I couldn't take the chance with his life, nor could I risk my life with him as a distraction. This would be tricky enough as it was.

I shook my head no and he turned his back on me, walking away silently.

260

ℰ ℰ ℰ

Before bed, I shaved my face as closely as I could. Fortunately, Matthew was not especially hirsute, and judging from the baby fine hairs, shaving might not have been necessary at all. I had almost as much facial hair when I was a woman.

Next, I made sure everything I needed was ready to go. My plan was to leave before anyone awakened, but in such close quarters, I wasn't sure it would be possible.

I expected sleep would be difficult if not impossible, but I employed an old trick of visualizing a black background and clearing my thoughts. It worked and I slept soundly until the need to urinate hit about six hours later.

All was quiet, so I eased away from Boy and dressed quickly. Minutes later, I closed the door softly and headed for the unoccupied common basement of the building we lived in.

Once there, I opened the first of the bundles George had prepared for me. Although temperatures hadn't dropped below freezing yet, it could happen any time now, so I redressed myself with long johns beneath my regular clothes, and double socks.

Then, I rolled up my trouser legs a bit and slid into the long cotton dress George provided. I'd hoped for a skirt and blouse, but George said the worn-looking round dress would serve my purposes well. The drop-shouldered yoke would mask my broader shoulders a bit, and the longer wide sleeve could allow me to conceal a weapon if need be. Moreover, the print and earth tones might provide camouflage in the woods.

Beggars can't be choosers. It was a nice loose fit, and the jacket he chose helped to further conceal my lack of breasts.

Next, I doubled a thick scarf and tied it over my head to cover my ears. I topped the scarf with a flat crowned straw hat that had a simple blue ribbon around it, tied in a bow at the back, and a wider ribbon that tied under the chin.

Finally, I laced up what George called a russet work shoe. The leather had a rough look to it, but the shoe was comfortable with my two pairs of socks. They were the only new item I wore but the design of the shoe did not make that obvious, and a mile or two on dirt roads would effectively obscure any trace of newness.

I put the compass and the heavy revolver George provided in my right jacket pocket, a hunting knife and a forged travel pass in the left pocket, and the extra rounds of ammo in the inside pocket.

Feeling good to go, I combined the remaining items from the two bundles into one and wore it as a makeshift backpack.

Of course, I realized I might be overpacking just a "tetch," as Mom used to say. My packing practices changed once I saw an interview with Amelia Earhart on public television that aired on the 50th anniversary of her rescue from a South Pacific atoll following her ill-fated around-the-world flight.

Earhart said she always obsessed over the weight in her aircraft, but a dear friend pressed, begged, and cajoled her to carry special radio equipment that would help ships locate her in the event of an emergency. Only at the last minute did she relent, and even then, she almost ditched the hardware in New Guinea. The rest is history.

So I tend to overpack. Better safe than sorry.

It was still dark as I started down the same road I'd followed Harriet down many months before, but a glance to my left showed traces of sunlight on the horizon.

Despite the perilousness, uncertainty, and overall downright stupidity of my venture, I couldn't help but smile about this being the first time I'd worn a dress in quite some time.

I felt pretty. Ha!

27

A Drag Race

Harriet Tubman told me that a woman attracts less suspicion than a man, and a woman heading South attracts less suspicion than a woman heading North.

For that reason I was moderately relaxed as I began my journey.

On foot, it takes a sizeable chunk of time just to get out of Philadelphia. If I were dumb enough to try this again, I'd definitely get someone to, at the very least, give me a ride to the edge of town or the state border.

I'd eaten an apple for breakfast and as I neared the edge of civilization, I stopped to fill my canteen and get out a bit of hardtack to snack on.

I turned to the water pump and I spotted a familiar figure scrambling to try to hide behind a post. After a deep sigh of annoyance, I counted to ten and focused on not exploding. I filled and repacked the canteen, drank my fill from the pump, and took out two pieces of hardtack.

"Come on out, Boy," I called to him, not masking my irritation.

He stuck out his head and then strolled toward me like he'd done nothing wrong.

I handed him a cracker, took a deep breath, and calmly but firmly told him, "You've got to go back home."

"Why?"

"I told you last night. This could be dangerous. I don't want to have to worry about you while I'm trying to free Mr. Thomas and Paula."

"I can help."

His desire to accompany me and to help was completely understandable. I'd certainly want to do the same if I were he. And if I took the time to take him back to the house, I'd lose half a day's light and my planned two-day hike would take three. Moreover, I'd be that much more at risk of hitting bad weather.

Chances were, he'd just try to follow me again and all the time spent taking him back would be wasted, plus he might get lost trying to track me down. Reluctantly, I decided to take him with me. Hopefully, a woman with a child would be even less suspicious to slave catchers.

I put my hands on his shoulders and focused on his face, hoping to make him fully grasp the gravity of what we were about to do.

"Listen carefully. You can come, *if* you promise to do exactly what I say as soon as I say it without asking why. If I say 'down,' just lie flat on the ground because I may have spotted someone with a gun about to shoot at us. If I say 'run,' move as fast as you can. Explanations can come later. We won't do Mr. Thomas and Paula any good if we get killed. Understand?"

"Yep. I understand," Boy said earnestly, nodding slowly. "But you look funny in a dress," he added.

All in all, it wasn't the most harebrained thing I'd done in this time period. At least I hoped it wouldn't be.

⚬ ⚬ ⚬

"Is you punishing me for following you?" Boy asked after we'd been walking for about an hour.

Instead of making conversation, I had started by asking him to spell a variety of words, but switched to math after I was satisfied his spelling was up to snuff.

"Do you remember why Mr. Bates sold us in the first place?" I asked.

"Yeah. Cause I could read."

"Why do think your reading made him want to sell us?"

"I don't know."

266

"Reading is power, kid," I said, sounding like a PBS children's show ad. "The better you learn to read and write and cipher, the more options you have in life. You won't have to do back-breaking labor in the tobacco fields. You can teach, or practice medicine, or be an accountant, or lots of other things."

"You really think I can do all that?"

"Definitely, as long as you continue to study. It won't be easy because you're a Negro and the deck is stacked against you, but I believe you can."

"So you not punishing me?" Boy asked in a skeptical tone. "You giving me power?"

"Exactly."

"The ciphering just feel like punishment," he moped.

"For now," I smiled. And proceeded to give him another problem to solve.

♀ ♀ ♀

We maintained a steady pace along the dirt road, just as I had with Harriet, keeping the Delaware River to our left.

To my surprise, I appreciated having Boy along for company. His presence kept my mind off of the dangers ahead, at least for as long as we were in Pennsylvania. Ideally, we would camp out near the Delaware border and enter Maryland the following night under cover of darkness.

My biggest concerns were food and water. I filled my canteen from outdoor pumps at every opportunity.

Just before dark the first night, we spied apple trees with a few apples that hadn't yet gone to worm. We gathered as many as we could carry and I relaxed, knowing they would provide both nutrition and hydration.

As the evening cooled, Boy began to slow and shiver. After finding a spot to sit, I gave him a blanket and extra socks from my pack.

I found myself looking for the general area where Harriet and I stopped our first night so many months ago, but eventually realized it was hopeless. I finally settled on a spot above the river with thick shrubbery and lots of dead leaves to sleep on. Based on the limited signage, we were either just inside the Delaware state line or at the edge of Pennsylvania.

I opted not to build a fire for fear of attracting unwanted attention, so Boy and I huddled together buried beneath a tarp, blankets and leaves for warmth. Although Boy's presence was unplanned, on that cool night it was much appreciated.

♪ ♪ ♪

At sunrise, we awakened remarkably refreshed, a natural benefit of our youth I suppose.

For as much as I missed my old life and feminine form, I am certain my former forty-something, big-boned body would not have responded nearly as well to a night of sleeping on the ground in near freezing weather.

After repacking the blankets and tarp, we immediately hit the road, stopping only to relieve ourselves. Hardly a day goes by that I don't wish for soft, two-ply toilet paper. George was sweet enough to pack the nineteenth century equivalent, but trust me, it's just not the same.

The next sign I saw indicated we had in fact spent the night in Delaware. Despite still having a full day of walking ahead of us, I felt optimistic.

We began practicing avoiding contact with passersby, mostly just for fun, by slipping into the woods or brush when we heard hoofbeats, or anything that might be other humans. Boy responded with the proper gravitas when I prompted him to hide.

Fortunately, Harriet was correct about how little attention we drew because we were going south. Whenever we passed through a small town, we refilled the canteen, nodded politely at others, and continued on our way.

As the sun began setting, we were still in Delaware, but just barely. I decided we'd best get off the main road before entering the more repressive slave state of Maryland. The road had taken us farther from the river, cutting across the state in a more direct path to Maryland. I recalled doing the same with Harriet and felt comfortable with our progress thus far.

Wending through the woods after dark was another matter, so we stayed parallel to the road for several more hours until we reached the turnoff for the plantations.

I had three possible routes to choose from for getting to the Bates plantation. The shortest and most exposed, and therefore most dangerous, would be to get back on the main road. Alternatively, we could walk through the empty, harvested tobacco fields of two other plantations or take an even more circuitous path through the woods. Despite the fact that the road was deserted, I decided it best to avoid it, and chose to cut through the fields.

The woods would probably be safest of all, but I didn't want to lose any more time. My master plan was to go get Mr. Thomas and Paula as soon as the lights went out in the cabins. That way, we could travel all night and easily be in Delaware before anyone noticed they were missing.

My ace in the hole involved drugging the dogs that might be used to track us.

George had obtained a sleeping powder called chloral hydrate from the apothecary. Before leaving, I mixed it with whiskey and generously laced some salt pork with the concoction, all sealed in a Mason jar. The trick would be approaching the dogs and feeding them before they sounded the alarm.

While I was still on the plantation, before being sold South, I had worked on an escape plan, part of which involved befriending the hounds. I'd occasionally slip them a bit of meat or bones, and it had gotten to the point where they produced a lovely Pavlovian drool when they smelled me approaching.

But would they still remember?

When Boy and I got close enough to see the big house and the cabins, the entire ground floor of the house was illuminated, as well as almost every cabin. All we could do was lie on the ground and wait.

We both dozed off almost immediately after our exertions of the day. When I started awake, only one light remained on in the big house, and it was upstairs. Flickering candlelight was still visible in the overseer's cabin and one slave cabin, but otherwise, things were quiet.

I considered leaving Boy asleep in the field while I gathered his father and sister, but decided his good behavior should be rewarded. I shook him awake and we silently crept to our former residence.

When we opened the door, all was dark except what the moonlight illuminated through the doorway.

Boy dashed over to his father's sleeping pallet, and then turned to me saying, "He ain't here. Neither is Paula."

28

When the Snafu Hits the Fan

Up to that point, everything had gone well. But this I hadn't figured on.

Had they been sold?

Had they already escaped?

Were they even alive?

My mind raced with the possibilities and panic took over for a long fifteen seconds.

Then Boy spoke up and matter-of-factly said, "Daddy probably at Brenda's cabin. I go get him."

Well don't kids say the darnedest things?

I exhaled and said, "Okay. Bring him back here. I'll be back in a few minutes."

As Boy slipped out of the cabin, I removed my pack and found the jar with the salt pork for the dogs.

272

Leaving the pack in the cabin, I worked my way in the shadows to the far side of the barn where the dogs were kenneled.

I had sealed the jar with paraffin back in Philly. Before I rounded the corner of the barn, I opened the jar so the smell of pork would reach the dogs around the same time my scent did.

Drool. They remembered.

I quickly fed each dog a chunk of drugged pork and crept back to the Thomas shack.

Boy and Mr. Thomas weren't back by the time I'd returned. Before I had time to really begin worrying, they came in, but with Brenda in tow.

As soon as they crossed the threshold, Brenda, in a loud whisper, began entreating Mr. Thomas to stay.

"When they catch you, they gone cut your feet. And you know you get the whip. It ain't worth it."

Seeing the potential for a clusterfuck of epic proportions, I whispered back, without fully thinking it through, "We won't get caught if we leave soon. Come with us, Brenda."

Mr. Thomas whipped his head toward me and flashed a look I never expected to see in his eyes — fear. Oops.

"You must be crazy, boy," she whisper-shouted at me. "I ain't built for no running, and them dogs would make two or three good meals outta me. I ain't no fool. And why you dressed like a woman anyway?"

Mr. Thomas again looked at me, this time with relief in his face, and then confusion as he scanned my appearance.

Of course Brenda was right about not being built for running. She was bigger-boned than I had ever been in my previous life, especially up top (and I certainly never needed to stuff my bra).

"I understand it's your choice, but please don't say anything. If we hurry, we can be out of Maryland before the sun rises. The dogs will still be sleeping for a few hours by the time we reach a free state. I made sure of that. Now where's Paula?"

Mr. Thomas and Brenda exchanged a series of looks, sort of a back and forth conversation, with raised eyebrows and head gestures, until Mr. Thomas finally conceded.

"Now see," he began slowly, "after you got sold off, Paula, she thought she was never gone see you again. So when Joseph started coming around, being all nice and all, after a while, she started spending time with him. He say he feel bad about getting Boy sold off —"

"Okay," I interrupted. "We've just got to find her and leave. Every extra minute we hang around here, the more likely we are to get caught. Where is she?"

"Prob'ly in the field past the last cabins over there," he said.

"Since Boy and I aren't supposed to be here, you should go get her."

He looked at Brenda and she nodded. Then he slipped out into the night.

Brenda then looked me up and down again, raised her eyebrows, smiled wryly, and silently asked me again about my outfit.

"Someone told me that women are less likely to be stopped and suspected of being runaways. Plus I didn't want to be recognized. Okay?"

"I forgot how funny you talk," Brenda sniggered, shaking her head from side to side. "If it work, it work. Just keep everybody safe, Matthew."

"I will," I responded seriously.

While we waited for Mr. Thomas to return, Brenda hugged the cringing Boy repeatedly, whispering about how happy she was to see him again and how glad she was that he was okay.

When Mr. Thomas finally returned, Paula was not with him. Instead he was hauling a clearly unwilling Joseph. Joseph, sporting a fresh black eye, was crying like a five-year-old whose puppy had just died.

"Now talk, boy!" Mr. Thomas ordered in a threatening whisper.

"I didn't want to say nothing because Mr. Jones might kill you, suh. Overseer caught us tonight and took Paula to his cabin. He hit me in the face and told me not to say nothing."

"What!?" Mr. Thomas roared, not bothering to whisper.

He spun to go to the door, but I blocked his path.

"Let me go," I said. Then I showed him my revolver.

"Not gonna need that," he growled through clenched teeth. "We both go."

I nodded, recognizing the need to keep things quiet, but keeping the gun in reserve in case the overseer was armed.

Boy, who had been silent up until then, piped in, "Me too."

Brenda, Mr. Thomas, and I turned to him, and whispered firmly in chorus, "No."

"Keep him here by any means necessary until we get back," I told Brenda. "He's sneaky."

"Don't worry 'bout us. Go!"

We quickly slid into the night and ran to the overseer's cabin. As we approached the entrance seconds later, we heard a squeal.

Mr. Thomas flung open the door and dashed inside with me right behind.

Paula was lying on the bed with her blouse ripped open and skirt completely off. Her eyes were at first wide with fear, and then relief at seeing her father. She did a triple-take at me, at first not recognizing me, and after realizing who I was, naturally wondering about my garb.

Jones was standing over her with his pants around his ankles, displaying a small turgid penis that almost

276

instantly contracted and withdrew into his bushy scrotum. His eyes took over Paula's expression of fear upon spying the formidable Mr. Thomas.

In two quick strides, Mr. Thomas reached the overseer. He struck him three quick blows to the chest with palm of his hand until Jones' back was against the far wall of the cabin. Then, with one powerful arm, he lifted Jones off the floor against the wall by the neck like he weighed nothing.

I spotted Paula's skirt on the floor and tossed it to her while following her father.

"I want . . . to pinch . . . his . . . head off, Matthew," Mr. Thomas said in a low growl, veins popping out on his face. He was just barely controlling his rage and seemed to be asking me for help.

I despise rapists and was only slightly less enraged. I've always felt that if more men were raped (by larger, stronger men, obviously, to make the experience comparable), they would understand the feeling of violation, and would finally take it more seriously.

"If we kill a White man, they'll never stop hunting for us," I began.

Then, gradually easing into my best diabolical smile, I slowly pulled out my large, single-edged hunting knife.

"However, if we cut off his little thing, maybe he'll think twice before he decides to report you missing," I concluded, mostly intending to frighten Jones.

Mostly.

Mr. Thomas continued to brace Jones against the wall as he thought about my proposal. Suddenly, he dropped Jones to the floor and began shaking with laughter.

His snickers were contagious, at least to me, and I began chuckling. Jones just squatted on the floor, looking down and probably hoping we would forget about him.

"Let's just go," Paula spoke up softly. "Please."

I think we'd both forgotten she was still there.

"Now you niggers better —" Jones blustered hoarsely, starting to speak while rising from the floor.

A massive blow from Mr. Thomas' fist to his jaw quickly silenced him.

Jones crumpled to the floor, bleeding from his cheek and mouth, and barely conscious.

"She's right," I said. "Let's tie up this worthless piece of, of . . . excrement and get going. If he says anything or tries to follow us, he dies first."

Then, turning to Jones, I reiterated, "I will not hesitate to end your miserable life if I ever see you again. Got it?"

He nodded shakily, but then a flicker of recognition showed in his now wide eyes.

"We s-s-sold you," he stammered.

"All the more reason for me to be displeased with you," I snarled, as I stroked his cheek with the side of my knife blade. "Now lie face down on the floor, asshole."

Once he was down, I put my knife away and removed his leather belt from his trousers, which were still around his ankles, while Mr. Thomas looked around for rope.

Before I could secure his legs, though, the cabin door opened and the plantation owner, Mr. Bates, entered, accompanied by Joseph and Joseph's father, the slave driver, Ole Sam. All three were out of breath. That weasel must have dashed straight to his father after we left Mr. Thomas' cabin.

Clusterfuck of epic proportions achieved.

Bates was holding a heavy-looking caplock pistol, which he straightaway aimed at Mr. Thomas. When he saw Jones on the floor with me standing over Jones' naked derrière, he barked, "Get up and pull on your trousers, man! What's going on here?"

Ever the suck-up, Ole Sam chimed in, saying, "Well, suh, like my boy was saying, these here niggers —"

"Not you, boy! Mr. Jones, tell me what on earth you are doing with your butt out in a cabin full of niggers?"

Excellent question.

I hoped Jones would fumble for words and distract Bates long enough for me to get my gun out. Unfortunately for me, Jones got straight to the point, talking hurriedly while getting dressed.

"The nigger in the dress is the nigger we sold a few months ago. He got a knife, and he come to get Mr. Thomas and this here gal and steal'em away."

Bates immediately turned his weapon to me, giving me a hard look.

"Damn you, nigger!" he cursed at me. "God help me, I should shoot you right here on the spot. If you weren't worth more to me alive . . ."

His voice trailed off as he sighed and shook his head from side to side. After a few seconds of thought, he announced, "What the hell. I'm gonna double my profits on you as soon as you heal from the beating Mr. Jones gives you."

I'd taken my eyes off of Jones while Bates spoke. When I looked back at him, he was holding an old single-shot handgun of his own. And, wearing a cruel smile, he pointed it right at my chest.

"That nigger ain't nothin' but trouble," he sneered. "I say we kill his black ass right now."

"Listen here, Jones," Bates began, in a tone intended to calm Jones, "that nigger is my property, and a dead nigger does not put money in my pocket. You are just going to have to settle for beating him to within an inch of his black life."

"He threatened to cut me," Jones spat at his boss, now focused more on Bates, and absently aiming his weapon more toward him too. The mixture of spittle and blood around his mouth made him look rabid, and even more dangerous than an angry man with a large gun would normally look.

280

Fearing I might not have a better opportunity, with my left hand, I motioned Paula and Mr. Thomas toward the door and out of the line of fire. At the same time, I eased my right hand into my jacket pocket to grip my revolver.

Jones and Bates were having a standoff, Jones glaring at his employer and Bates now slowly easing his pistol in Jones' direction.

"I pay your salary, Mr. Jones, and you will do as I say," Bates insisted, not taking his eyes off his enraged overseer.

The way things were going, they might shoot one another, and save me the trouble. On the other hand, Jones might just as likely execute me.

I took aim at Jones as best I could through my pocket and fired one shot.

Almost instantly upon hearing the blast of my gun, Bates shot Jones, thinking Jones had fired at him.

At the same time, Jones, of the same mindset, grunted in pain and fired at Bates.

Smoke clouded the area around both men for a few seconds before rising as the men slumped to the floor.

Jones was clearly DRT, as my brother used to say. Dead right there.

Ole Sam was on his knees cradling Bates' head and cooing over him.

I turned to Mr. Thomas and Paula, and told them to go back to Boy and Brenda to let them know we were okay. Three gunshots would certainly have them both concerned and frightened.

Next, I approached Bates, Ole Sam, and Joseph. Bates' left shoulder was bleeding profusely.

The first thing Bates said to me when he looked up at me was, "Damned smart ass nigger."

"You're losing a pretty good amount of blood," I said, ignoring his gibe. "Sam, Joseph, sit him up on the bed. That should slow the blood flow and keep him from passing out."

While they did that, I found a cloth that I moistened with what looked like liquor. I ripped open his shirt to expose the wound. The ball from the pistol had slashed through the deltoid and taken out a fair-sized chunk of muscle.

I pressed the wet cloth firmly on the wound, causing Bates to wince and his eyes to tear up.

"Joseph!" I called. "Hold this as tightly as you can. That will stem the bleeding, and ideally help seal the wound."

Joseph looked at his father, and then at Bates. Bates nodded.

"I only know rudimentary first aid," I told Bates, "but fortunately for you, this wound is pretty straightforward. My guess is, unless it gets infected, you should recover just fine, assuming you don't lose too much blood. That's why I have you sitting up and Joseph applying pressure to the wound. Do you have alcohol in the house? We've got to clean the wound site."

"Yes," he said softly. "Sam. Please tell my wife what happened and she will get the alcohol. Tell her to send for the doctor too."

"Yassuh Massuh Bates."

Ole Sam skipped out of the door, happy to serve.

"Why are you helping me, boy?" Bates asked me quietly.

"You know my escape would be easier, far easier, with you dead or dying. But I'm not an animal, despite you treating me as one."

My remark let him know his life was in my hands and that I was allowing him to live.

Bates rested his head on his right hand and massaged his temple. Then he looked up, took a deep breath, and, shaking his head from left to right, spoke.

"Confound it, boy! I knew you were trouble that first time I heard you speak. But I just could not pass up the chance to own a young buck in his prime for free. And this is my punishment."

"Perhaps. But what you fail to comprehend is, while you may have enslaved me, sir, you never owned me."

Bates looked down, avoiding my eyes.

"I'm leaving now," I told Bates, handing him Jones' bottle of liquor. "Take a swig or two to dull the pain. Hopefully we won't meet again."

Bates sighed, and then nodded in resignation.

I took that as a gentlemen's agreement, realizing he might change his mind once he saw that I had in fact taken both Mr. Thomas and Paula.

I turned to leave, but looked back and caught Joseph's eye. Bates' head was still down.

I put a finger to my lips, requesting he keep quiet about Mr. Thomas and Paula. He too nodded.

It was a calculated risk to allow Bates to live, and Joseph too, for that matter. I figured that by the time a doctor treated him and the dogs awakened from their drug-induced sleep, we would be in Delaware. Without an overseer, by the time he ascertained I hadn't left alone, unless Joseph talked, we'd be in Pennsylvania.

And if Bates figured out that Jones had a second bullet wound not caused by himself, he would also figure out that I could have shot him too.

My hope was that 'Massuh' had seen enough of me to last a lifetime. I knew for certain that I'd seen enough bloodshed.

29

On the Road Again

I hurried back to gather Mr. Thomas, Paula and Boy. They had already put on tattered jackets and were packing small bundles. After retrieving my pack and reloading my pistol, I motioned for them to follow me.

I moved to exit but Brenda had blocked the door. She gave each of the Thomas children a warm hug, and gave Mr. Thomas a more heated embrace and lingering kiss. Then she inclined her head to me, her eyes and raised eyebrows reminding me to take care of them.

"Now you all wait here just one minute," Brenda ordered. "Let me get you something to eat. I be right back."

She was gone closer to three minutes, but returned with a small cloth bundle that she gave to Paula.

"Now everybody wondering what going on," she told us. "Y'all wait a minute 'til they come 'round me, and then go. No need for everybody to know everything what happening."

Smart woman.

♂ ♂ ♂

I led the way, with Mr. Thomas as rear guard. Again I cut through the harvested tobacco fields to save time. Then it was back into the woods, parallel to the road. Since we'd just come this way, I wasn't worried about getting lost.

"Hold up," Mr. Thomas said as he jogged up to my position. "Listen."

We all stopped and concentrated on the crackling sounds behind us.

"Paula, Boy, go up ahead a little and hide behind those big trees," I ordered. "Mr. Thomas. Are you good with hanging right here in the clearing while I circle around behind whoever it is?"

He nodded.

I disappeared into the shadows and pulled out my knife. No need to make more noise than necessary.

As soon as the footsteps passed my location, Mr. Thomas grunted, "Hey."

When our stalker looked toward Mr. Thomas, I crept behind him, grabbing his chin with my left hand, and exposing his neck to the knife I held in my right.

Almost immediately, I knew it was Joseph.

"What the fuck, Joseph?" I asked angrily, not releasing him. My time on the police force had definitely increased my propensity to use colorful language in times of stress.

No answer was forthcoming to my inarticulate query, partly because 'fuck' was not in the trembling young man's vocabulary. I suspect the knife to his throat also contributed to his elective mutism.

"Let the boy go, Matthew," Mr. Thomas said wearily. "What you want, boy?"

"I wants to come with you," Joseph exhaled. "And, and be with Paula."

Paula and Boy came out of hiding. She half smiled, but stayed behind her father.

"Did anyone follow you?" I asked irritably, still disgusted with him for getting Bates involved earlier. "Because if anyone follows us, I will shoot you first."

I made a point of staring him down when I said it. His cowed expression indicated he believed me.

"Don't waste no bullet on that boy," Mr. Thomas calmly intoned. "I just squeeze the life out of him. Save your bullets for the men with the guns."

Made sense.

"Who knows you're gone?" I asked.

"Just Daddy."

"Damn. Damn! Ole Sam's probably already told Bates."

"No. Daddy say he gone play dumb and ain't gone say nothing. He know I just want to be with Paula."

"I don't know. He sure seems to love Bates."

"He love me more," Joseph said firmly. "He only so close to Massuh Bates 'cause they got the same daddy."

"They're half-brothers?" I asked incredulously.

"Yeah, but we can't never say nothing about it. Daddy told me somebody say something about it when he was a boy, and the old Massuh Bates got'em whipped and sold South."

Mr. Thomas and I exchanged a glance, and he announced, "Well just in case your daddy don't keep his mouth shut, we best keep moving."

I hustled back into the lead with Joseph and Paula behind me, and Mr. Thomas with Boy again at the rear.

♪ ♪ ♪

Less than two hours later, we'd crossed into Delaware. According to William Still, Delaware was ostensibly a slave state, but close to ninety percent of all Blacks living there were free. The largest slave owner in the state had fewer than twenty slaves. Free Blacks were the norm, so we wouldn't be too out of place. However, roaming slave catchers might try to roust us, so it was best to stay out of sight.

Paula, Boy and Joseph were slowing and obviously tired, but I didn't want to gamble our safety by resting too close to the border. No one complained, so I forged ahead.

288

By the time the sun was rising, we'd traversed far enough into the state, and far enough from populated areas, that I felt comfortable taking a break. I spread a tarp on a soft and leafy, but sheltered, spot and we all collapsed.

Mr. Thomas slept on one side of Paula, with Boy on the other, leaving Joseph next to me. I still didn't completely trust him and refused to relax until I heard his steady breathing.

When I awoke, Joseph was lightly snoring. Paula and Boy were also still snoozing, but Mr. Thomas was gone. I needed to 'drain the snake,' as my brother Eliot used to say before he matured enough to use the more genteel expression of 'take a leak.' Back then, I thought it pretty crude, but the longer I spent as a male, the more I sort of see the humor. Was I slowly becoming a man, I wondered?

Ugh.

Mr. Thomas apparently had the same urge. He came upon me a short distance from our camp, and waited until I finished to walk back with me.

"I appreciate you coming back for us, and for taking care of Boy," he said as we walked.

My mind filled with things to say in return, but I knew the correct manly response, so I just looked at him and nodded.

We roused the youngsters and gave them a few minutes to relieve themselves before hitting the road again.

Paula unwrapped the bundle Brenda had prepared for us, and handed out cornbread and bits of undrugged salt pork to each of us as we trekked through the woods. I passed around my canteen after we'd finished eating. I'd refilled it and the thoroughly rinsed Mason jar at the plantation. I didn't think to suggest that we ration the water and was shocked when Joseph tapped me on the shoulder with the empty vessel.

"You got any mo'?" he asked, sounding like a less refined Oliver Twist.

When I planned this expedition, I was going South alone and returning with two others. Instead, I was now traveling with a party of five. We might have made it to Pennsylvania without having to refill my water containers even with the two extra bodies, but there was no way to avoid replenishing our supply with Joseph acting as if a tap were around the corner.

I scowled at him and gave no reply as I snatched the canteen. In silence, I picked up the pace through the woods.

After about thirty minutes, Paula skipped up to join me, leaving Joseph behind with Mr. Thomas and Boy.

"You mad at me?" she asked softly.

At first, I wasn't sure what she meant, but then I realized she was referring to her relationship with Joseph.

290

"No," I replied, looking into her eyes and flashing a tiny, forced smile.

"You seem like you real mad at Joseph."

"I am mad at him. He could have gotten us all killed, telling his father about us. And, to be frank, he's not good enough for you."

She was silent for a bit, considering what I'd said.

Finally, Paula said, "I didn't think you was gonna to come back. And Joseph, he always liked me. He just didn't know how to tell me. I always thought me and him was gonna to be together up till I met you. But you not like us. Joseph more like me, and he not so bad when we by ourselfs."

When I recalled the time I'd spent alone with Paula, my body responded in the usual manner of a teenaged boy. But I never intended to pursue her. I just didn't want her to be stuck with a jerk because he was the only guy around her age.

"I still don't like the guy, but if he makes you happy, I'll try not to kill him. If he ever mistreats you though, tell your father or me. Don't put up with it. You deserve a good man."

"Joseph ain't smart as you, but he ain't stupid. He know Daddy would break him into little pieces if he ever do me wrong."

She gave me a beautiful smile, kissed my cheek, and drifted back with her family, leaving me to wonder about my future here in the past. I felt a real connection with

Caroline, but would I ever be able to have a real and honest relationship? A romantic relationship. Would that even be a good idea?

I pushed on, contemplating my absurd situation while making certain we were heading in the right direction.

After a couple of more hours of walking, I became aware of more activity to our left, so I led us farther in the woods to avoid contact with other people. It was time for a quick break, but I realized we had no water.

Since Boy and I had stopped for water on the way South, I decided to try it again. We would leave the others behind, as their outfits screamed runaway.

He and I strolled out of the woods and into the small town like we belonged there. The water pump was just outside the general store.

As I finished filling my canteen and Mason jar, luck seemed to still be with us, right up until two men wearing badges approached us.

The older of the two had a thick moustache and he nodded to us, saying, "How do? You all new around here?"

"We are fine. Just passing through, sir," I replied in a falsetto befitting my feminine garb, and glad that I sounded nothing like a slave.

I'd been told that Delaware was comparatively reasonable in its treatment of Blacks, and that it was one of the least oppressive of the states that allowed human beings to be held as property and treated as subhuman (a

292

low bar, to be sure). Nevertheless, I had finally figured out that being Black anywhere meant walking a tightrope, and I knew I had to be very careful where I stepped.

"Where you all headed?" he followed up.

"Philadelphia, sir."

"What are you doing hereabouts?"

"Well, sir," I began slowly, trying to sound relaxed with my fabrication, "our daddy works on the docks, but sometimes there's no work, so we came looking for day work to help out the family."

The older lawman bowed his head once, tipped his hat, and said, "Well good luck, ma'am."

Satisfied with my story, he was ready to move along.

The younger peacekeeper, however, spoke up next, asking, "How do we know you all not runaways?"

He was clearly the more suspicious and less easygoing of the two, eyeing us through narrowed lids.

"Well, sir," I replied politely, "I never met any runaways, but how many runaways do you know who go to school and complain about it all the time like him?"

I pointed at Boy, who shrugged but maintained his cool.

"Is that true, boy," the older man asked, "that you don't like school?"

"Well sir," Boy began, "I likes reading and writing just fine, but I hates ciphering."

Eager to catch us in a lie, the younger man promptly asked Boy "What is nine plus nine?"

"Well that is eighteen sir," Boy replied swiftly. "Them kind of problems is easy. What I hates is carrying and borrowing."

The older man smiled and then chuckled, reluctantly joined by the younger man seconds later when he realized his boss had no misgivings whatsoever about our story.

"What's your name, boy?" the elder gentleman asked, still smiling.

Damn! So close, I thought. When Boy tells him his name, the sheriff will ask why his parents named him Boy, and then it's game over, man.

I flashed Boy a look that I hoped said, "Lie through your teeth and make up a name, any name except Boy!"

"Thomas, sir," Boy replied smoothly.

"How do you spell that?"

"T-h-a-t, that."

"He can't spell his own name?" the young deputy challenged, suspicions again aroused.

This time it was my turn to smile.

"He can," I said, "but he thought you were asking him to spell the word 'that,' sir. We play a spelling game so he's accustomed to spelling the exact word I say."

"Now that's funny," the sheriff chortled. "I'll have to try that one on my young'uns."

Then he looked down into Boy's face with a grin, saying, "And Thomas, I know exactly what you mean about that ciphering."

The older man then motioned with his head to his companion to continue on their way.

As they walked away from us, I heard the younger guy mutter, "Damn, that is one homely gal."

"Well done," I whispered to Boy.

30

There's No Place Like Home

Incredibly, on a trip where so much could have gone wrong, and so much did in fact go wrong, we safely crossed the Pennsylvania border a few hours after sundown. We'd been moving at a smart pace all day long and still had several hours more to travel before reaching my home in Philadelphia. Except for Mr. Thomas, we were all dragging from exhaustion, so we decided to camp again.

A light snow began falling as we arranged one of my blankets overhead like a tarp and made a mattress of leaves beneath the actual tarp on the ground. The temperature had begun to drop hours ago, but we hadn't felt it much because of our activity level.

Now that we were in Pennsylvania, I decided to give my dress to Paula for warmth, but I kept the scarf I was wearing on my head to protect my ears. Boy, or should I say Thomas, was groggily amused at the sight of me removing the dress.

Paula again slept between Mr. Thomas and Boy, but this time Joseph was on the other side of Mr. Thomas while I snuggled next to Boy.

Just before we fell asleep, Mr. Thomas asked softly, "That all we had to do to be free?"

"In a way," I replied, "but you're not truly safe here. The Fugitive Slave Act can still be used to capture you and take you back. We have to go farther and probably get you a new identity, or maybe get you to Canada. My boss will know more. Anyway, that's why they don't want you to learn to read – so you won't be able to do for yourself."

When I stopped rambling on, I could tell everyone else had already slipped into dreamland, so I shut my eyes and my mouth and joined them.

ᘓ ᘓ ᘓ

I don't know what time it was when I heard Mr. Thomas stirring, but it felt like the right time to get back on the road home. If I had to guess, I'd reckon it to be about 3:00 a.m. The moon was still fairly high in the sky and the sun was nowhere to be seen.

I passed the water around after everyone had the opportunity to relieve themselves. Then we hit the trail with me in front again and Mr. Thomas watching our rear, all of us nibbling on the last bits of hardtack.

The sun had been up for a few hours by the time I recognized the road to William Still's offices. I was counting on his Underground Railroad connections to shelter and protect the Thomas family and Joseph.

I led them to the rear entrance, making sure we were not seen, and secured the door behind us.

"Wait here while I get Mr. Still," I told my companions.

Still was in the front office hunched over paperwork as usual, but he turned when he heard me enter.

"Success, young friend?" he asked with a serious expression.

"Yes. They're in the warehouse."

"I would suppose there is much to tell, but you should go home and rest. I will contact the Vigilance Committee regarding your fellow travelers."

"Thank you. I'll say goodbye on the way out."

Although I'd known this moment would come, I suddenly realized that I was closer to Mr. Thomas and his family than to Matthew's family. I would really miss them.

I'd never had children of my own or a younger sibling. As an elementary school teacher, I felt like I had shared custody of a gaggle of kids. Quiet evenings at home were exactly what I needed to recover from a day in the classroom and recharge me for the following day in the classroom. Thus, I never felt like I was missing something in my life.

The time I'd spent with Boy and Oleta made me wonder if I should have considered parenthood.

Paula didn't feel like a sister or daughter though, and clearly Mr. Thomas wasn't a spousal substitute. They were just familiar, comfortable friends in a time where I felt out of place and often alone.

"I guess this is goodbye," I began.

Boy and Paula wrapped themselves around me and squeezed for all they were worth.

Paula let go first, giving me a quick peck on the lips and a disturbingly seductive grin before backing off to rejoin a clearly agitated Joseph. He grabbed her hand and pulled her to him, trying to appear triumphant but actually just looking confused.

Women!

"Don't worry about me studying, Matthew," Boy said. "I know it's important."

He and I had been through so much together. I loved him, and hated that I might never see him again.

I pulled him to me again and got on my knees to hug him. As I clutched the child tightly, I whispered to him, "I know you'll study hard. You know too much not to."

As Mr. Thomas approached with his massive mitt outstretched, Boy drifted away.

I stood and we shook hands firmly. Then Mr. Thomas looked me in the eye and said softly, "I really ain't expect you to come back. I ain't even think you could, but you did. You a good man, Matthew, and I am proud to call you my friend."

"Thank you, sir. I feel the same way. Good luck, and take care. Maybe we'll meet again someday."

"I hope so. I truly do."

We had shared a moment that would normally end in an embrace, except of course, real men don't hug. I wasn't quite there yet as a man, so I had to fight the urge.

I knew I needed to leave quickly or I would cry, which is really taboo for manly men of our ilk. I gave each one a last nod, including Joseph, and walked out practically dry-eyed.

Finally, I began the last leg of my long journey back to Walnut Street and what I finally accepted would be my home for a long time to come.

Epilogue

A few weeks later, on December 2, 1859, John Brown was hanged in Virginia.

The following November, Abraham Lincoln was elected President. Within days, even before Lincoln was inaugurated in March, South Carolina seceded from the Union, followed by Mississippi, Florida, Alabama, Georgia, Louisiana, and Texas over the next few weeks.

The month after Lincoln's inauguration, the new Confederacy fired on Fort Sumter in Charleston Harbor, beginning a horrific war far beyond anything I could have imagined.

As the years pass, I've gotten to the point that I don't think about what I have wrought for days at a time.

But to anyone who reads this, please learn from my mistake. My interactions with Tubman and Brown inadvertently led to a brutal war.

On the one hand, one could argue that in the end, nearly four million Black men, women, and children are enjoying freedom thirty-five years earlier than they would have otherwise.

On the other hand, the price for that freedom was inordinately high. Moreover, tensions still remain high between the North and the South, as well as between Blacks and Whites.

Today, the 15th Amendment to the United States Constitution was ratified, giving Black men the right to vote. And just last month, a Black man from Mississippi was sworn into the U.S. Senate.

Maybe John Brown was right, and things will be better in this timeline. Maybe I will, at some point, forgive myself.

These days, I focus on being the best husband I can to my darling Caroline, and the best father I can to our two adopted children. Apparently, whatever killed the original Matthew Little left me sterile.

Our courtship was not smooth. At times, I pulled away because I didn't feel I deserved happiness, or because I felt I couldn't truly make her happy. At other times, she pulled away because she felt I was hiding something.

Oleta ultimately gave me the one piece of advice I needed to hear. She told me to stop being Eleanor and just be Matthew. She also advised me to never tell Caroline about Eleanor. Caroline would just think I was crazy. Oleta said the only reason she believed me was because of her youth at the time, and that she knew the former Matthew so well before he died.

Caroline and I both served as nurses during the war. At our hospital, we treated Union and Rebel soldiers. In the beginning, whenever a Reb would tell me not to touch him, I would try to persuade him to allow me to help. Eventually, though, I would just look at him sadly, say, "Rest in peace," and move on to the next patient. There was always a next patient.

Ultimately, after all the horrors we'd encountered, Caroline and I both realized that we loved and needed each other too much be apart. Together, everything else would work out. And it has.

Matthew Little
March 30, 1870

Afterword

About a year ago, the U.S. Postal Service delivered a somewhat large and heavy box to me from Wells Fargo. I wasn't expecting anything, but my name was plainly printed on the label, so I opened it.

Inside the box lay a package wrapped in really old, plain, brown paper addressed to an Eleanor Louise Ross. A sticky note read, "Unable to Locate – Deliver to Lennox Randon."

Weird, I thought. Why would Wells Fargo list me as a secondary recipient for a parcel intended for a woman I never met?

Underneath the outer wrapping of the package was a second layer of brown paper. This paper was heavy, thicker than a grocery bag, and even older looking than the first layer. The address had faded to near illegibility, but what I could make of it corresponded to the woman's address on the outer layer. Clearly, the package had been rewrapped over time as the paper deteriorated.

Knowing a mystery when I saw one, I meticulously removed that second layer, thinking it might be important for something at a later time. I gave no real thought to what the something might be because the next layer beckoned.

That final stratum was likely the first to enclose the package's contents, but those paper fragments could no longer make that claim. The material was so dark in color that it appeared to have been burnt, and lacked any discernible writing. It more or less disintegrated at my touch. *Freaky.* I decided to save the flaky residue, perhaps for carbon dating or some other such test.

The prize revealed beneath the layers of wrapping paper at first looked to be nothing more than a large block of murky wax, like from a bunch of melted candles. Upon closer examination, though, I could see something sealed within the wax. I briefly considered carefully melting the wax to reach the contents, but curiosity and impatience got the better of me. Instead, I grabbed the heftiest knife from the wood block in my kitchen and started carving.

In no time flat, I was in possession of a sealed envelope and several mint condition, old-fashioned lined notebooks that seemed to have been used as journals.

I began by opening the envelope and reading the letter that begins this book.

Utterly intrigued, I picked up the notebook with the oldest date on it and commenced reading.

A few hours later, I'd finished reading the first notebook. Based on what I'd read, I knew how I'd be spending the remainder of my week. On the first reading, certain things in the manuscript made no sense, until, all of a sudden, they made perfect sense.

By the time I'd read all of the notebooks, I realized that I believed every word. Like someone who is convinced of the existence of UFOs and little green men, though, I am loath to admit it. I have chosen to publish this as a work of fiction, but only because I have no definitive proof that it is true. True or not, I found it an interesting tale.

Among the most compelling of the facts leading me to accept the contents of the notebooks is that no agent or author has demanded fees, points, or anything at all.

The memoir arrived untitled, so I employed an apt phrase of the author's to serve that purpose. I think she would approve.

Curious as to why the package came to me, of all people, I called Wells Fargo and eventually tracked down the employee who'd forwarded it to me.

He was happy to speak with me and said he'd wondered what was in the parcel. He explained that Wells Fargo had been out of the delivery business for nearly a hundred years, so the box languished in storage until he and a co-worker happened upon it while organizing a warehouse.

The instructions with the package had a list of recipients, with my name fourth on the list. The other three names did not pan out, but I was the only Lennox Randon on the planet.

Just prior to publication of this book, I tracked down an old friend from high school, Robert Ross, Jr. We hadn't spoken since our 20-year reunion, but we'd been fairly close in school.

After giving him a quick explanation about the odd package I'd received, I asked if he had a twin sister or other relative by the name of Eleanor Ross. He replied that he was pretty sure he'd know if he had a twin sister, but would ask his parents about other relatives.

Robert called back a few days later to say that his parents told him a story he'd never heard.

At the time of his birth, his mother had been pregnant with twins. She and her husband had planned to name them Eliot and Eleanor, after Eliot Ness and Eleanor Roosevelt. Sadly, the female twin was stillborn, so they named him Robert, after his father instead.

I guess, most of all, that's why I believe.

Lennox Randon

About the Author

Lennox Randon is a graduate of the Houston Police Academy and The University of Texas at Austin, and has worked as a police officer, an elementary schoolteacher, and a technical writer.

As of this writing, Randon is living with metastatic GIST cancer.

Though born and raised in Texas, Randon currently resides in Iowa.

Randon is also the author of *Friends Dogs Bullets Lovers*.

www.LennoxRandon.com

www.facebook.com/LennoxRandonAuthor

Special thanks to Cindy Shoemaker Clayton, Lileah Harris, Wilbert Watkins, Rob Cline & Dennis Green for their invaluable first impressions.